THE —
PAINTED HORSE

Jenny Hughes

KENILWORTH PRESS

For my sister, Myra Hayles

Also by Jenny Hughes:
The Dark Horse
A Horse by Any Other Name

Published by Kenilworth Press Ltd
Addington, Buckingham MK18 2JR

© Jenny Hughes 2000

British Library Cataloguing in Publication Data
A catalogue record for this book is available from the British Library

ISBN 1-872119-21-2

Printed and bound in Great Britain by
Hillman Printers (Frome) Ltd

CHAPTER ONE

A T FIRST it was sheer exhilaration. The long track leading to the downs was covered in short, springy turf, sweeping gradually uphill, the perfect place for a gallop.

Diablo had been prancing and jogging the whole ride, nearly pulling my arms out of their sockets in his eagerness. So when I saw the path I just let him go. If you'd asked me in those days what were the aids for gallop I'd have looked blank and said "loosen the reins?" The way I rode Diablo it was as basic as that. I merely released my grip slightly and the big black horse was off like a rocket. Usually if I pointed him uphill, especially a steepish one, he'd be reasonably easy to stop at the top, but this was the first time we'd found this gentler slope and he wasn't going to waste the opportunity.

It was like flying, I thought, laughing as the wind whipped through my hair, revelling in the feel of all that speed and power beneath me. When the track began to level I asked the horse to slow, (which means I leant back and yelled *"whoa"* a few times). Diablo was having far too much fun and totally ignored it. No, I lie. I think it made him go faster. We thundered across the top of the downs, thankfully deserted now all the holidaymakers had gone, with me hauling ineffectually on the reins and starting to panic. The ground began to drop away quite sharply, but Diablo merely checked his stride a little, changed legs in mid-air and continued his mad flight. There were trees now, clawing and scratching at me as we raced headlong, and an evil looking ditch snaked alongside the path to my right.

The black horse wasn't paying attention to anything. Ignoring my puny attempts to make him stop, he was just galloping for the sheer hell of it, and only the purest luck kept him from dropping a foot into the ditch or crashing to his knees over a tree root. The trees thinned, the path widened, and I could at last see what was ahead – a reasonably flat, broad track curving round the bottom of the downs. No visible danger, and surely the manic creature I was riding would soon begin to tire and stop of his own accord?

My face was wet and my eyes stinging, whether with tears or blood from the scratches I couldn't tell, and my heart was pounding with fright. I tried once again to slow the pace down, but Diablo tossed his head as if in defiance and galloped relentlessly on. As we rounded the next bend I saw it – directly ahead of us the line of hedgerow was broken by a gap, a wide break which led directly on to the road. I could even hear the rumble of traffic and I knew, I just knew – the horse, seeking home, would at any second be streaking mindlessly, terrifyingly through that gap. At that point I should have bailed out, I suppose, simply thrown myself out of the saddle and onto the turf, but I had to try to turn him, to bring his head round somehow, and steer him away from the menacing roar of cars and lorries.

I heaved with all my strength on the opposite rein, seeing the gleam of his eye as his head turned slightly. But it was no good, the track led directly to the gap and Diablo, seemingly determined on a flat out gallop all the way home, was heading straight for it. I felt sick, my arms and legs were like jelly and I could hear the rush of blood pounding in my ears.

A tall figure appeared suddenly in the break of shrubs. He stood his ground firmly, legs astride and arms flailing, shouting "GET out of it. Go-oo on! Go-oo on!"

For the first time Diablo slowed visibly, wavered, then, unwilling to plunge forwards and cannon into the unexpected and forceful presence blocking his path, veered sharply away. My poor, soggy arms and legs promptly gave up and I and the big black horse parted company at last. I shot straight out of the side door and landed in the thickest, and of course the prickliest, of bushes edging the side of the road. Jabbed and battered by a thousand barbed branches I crawled out to see

Diablo standing quietly nearby, sides heaving as he allowed the tall figure to approach.

This was a young man, or boy, of about my own age, I saw now. He had thick, fair hair, grey eyes and wouldn't look out of place on a poster on your bedroom wall. I smiled weakly, conscious of looking less than my best, and pushed the tangle of curls out of my eyes.

"Typical. Look at him standing there like a pet lamb while you catch him. I could kill that horse sometimes."

"It's a complete wonder to me you haven't both killed each other before now." The irritation in his voice took me by surprise. "And this time, what's worse is that you could have hurt a lot of innocent motorists doing it. If you'd hit that road there'd have been a major accident, Lord knows how many people would have been injured. Just what the hell do you think you were playing at?"

I'd just been run away with, scratched, battered, bruised and generally mangled and now this complete stranger was YELLING at me.

"I didn't mean it to happen," I snapped defensively. "Diablo bolted and – "

"Why? Did something frighten him?" He was running his hands in an expert looking way over the horse's legs.

"No, I – I just let him have a gallop up the hill and then I couldn't stop him."

I knew it sounded weak but again I wasn't prepared for the venomous look he shot me from those steel grey eyes.

"Why not? What are you doing out on your own if you can't ride properly? Look at you. You aren't even wearing a decent hat."

I'd removed the ancient velvet cap I wear, and shaken out my dark curly hair in an effort to look more alluring. It obviously hadn't done the trick.

"I can ride," I said hotly. "I've had my own pony since I was ten. And I hate wearing a hat. I only put this one on because my dad won't let me out if I don't."

"Ye gods," he said quietly. "Well, you've had a lucky escape this time. Your horse seems none the worse. What about you?"

"I thought you'd never ask." I was still rankling at the "can't ride" jibe. "My leg hurts." I took a couple of steps very gingerly. "*Ow*. Oh, and there's blood all over my hands. You're sure Diablo's all right? He's not bleeding is he?"

"I've checked." The grey eyes looked briefly into mine. "It's probably from your face. It's all scratched to hell."

I fumbled for a tissue, wincing at the pain that shot through my leg. "I – I don't think I can make it home." I fished around in my other pocket. "Look, here's my phone card. Would you ring my house and tell them to send a car and trailer for us?

7

I don't know exactly where we are but – "

"You're on the edge of the downs the side that borders the dual carriageway from Hembury to Barringford." He was still unsmiling, unsympathetic. "It's only two or three miles to your house via the bridle paths but at least seven by road. And you're on the wrong side of the carriageway of course. Whoever 'came to fetch you' would have to go right up to the next junction and back again."

"So what do you suggest?" He was really annoying me now. "That I walk? Hop would be more like it. I can't put my foot to the floor."

"Diablo can. I told you he's perfectly all right."

"You expect me to RIDE?" I was flabbergasted. "I couldn't hold him before when I was fully fit, so-"

"I thought you said you knew how to ride. For someone who's had her own pony for three or four years – "

"Five years. Five and a half years." I could interrupt too. "I told you, he bolted and – "

"There's no way a properly schooled horse ridden by a competent rider should ever bolt in the circumstances you described." He was worse than unbearable. "And as for hobbling around grizzling and expecting everyone to rush out and rescue you – again, no way."

Tears of anger and frustration mingled unbeautifully with the blood on my face. "So you

8

think I should somehow climb back aboard this maniac and ride all the way back home?"

"He doesn't look like a maniac to me." He pulled Diablo's ears gently. "Just over eager and under trained. You should remember the old saying "if things go wrong it's always your fault not the horse's."

"But I don't think I can ride." I sniffed miserably. "My leg's hurting and if he takes off again...." Just the thought was enough to bring tears of self pity to my already brimming eyes.

"He won't. Come on, I'll give you a leg up." He walked the horse forward and before I knew it I was neatly propelled into the saddle.

For a moment I thought I'd pass out and fall immediately off again but I took a deep breath and tried to control my terror.

"All right?" The cool grey eyes were a little warmer, I thought.

I nodded and gathered up the reins with shaky fingers.

"Good girl. You probably think it's old fashioned, but it really is better to get straight back on after a fall if you possibly can."

I nodded again. The thought of riding Diablo all the way back was still so frightening I'd lost the power of speech. I squeezed my legs gently and the black horse moved away at a sedate walk.

I made a huge effort and said stiffly, "Thank you

very much for your help. I'll be OK now."

"Well done." He smiled for the first time, a devastating grin that nearly knocked me out of the saddle again.

"Oh," I felt utterly stupid. "No, I won't. I don't know how to get home from here. I've never been this way before."

"I'm walking your way. We'll show you, won't we, Jack?"

I hadn't spotted the dog a glossy border collie with a sharply intelligent face and a plumy tail that wagged immediately he heard his name.

"Thank you," I said it with a lot more sincerity this time, then did a double take. "But you don't know where my house is do you? I'm Stacey – "

"Stacey Jennings, and you live at Deepdene Manor."

"Oh!" I was genuinely surprised. "We haven't been here long and I don't know anyone yet. Er – what's your name then?"

"Dean." He hesitated and I saw his mouth tighten in a firm line. "I don't suppose I need say my surname. You'll have been warned about me even if you haven't met many of the locals."

"Warned?" Without realising I'd relaxed my tensed muscles and Diablo had stopped his usual jig-jogging and was walking beautifully. "Why should anyone tell us anything about you?"

"Your dad will be told to keep you away from

me because I'm bad news."

"Well he hasn't, and if he had, he wouldn't, and if he did, I shouldn't take any notice," I said incoherently. "I never do."

"Mm." Dean said it without enthusiasm. "You shouldn't be proud of that. It's a typical spoilt rich brat thing. You should listen to your parents. I bet they wanted you to have proper riding lessons instead of tearing around completely out of control on this perfectly good horse."

The perfectly good horse rolled an eye and began jogging sideways.

"How dare you!" I spluttered and tried to bring Diablo back to walk. "I am not spoilt or a brat and I do know how to ride."

"Sit properly then and stop tensing up. Give him a looser rein, and make your hands softer. If you strung up an old cart horse like that and perched on top like a coiled spring you'd make even him dance a bit."

I swallowed my fury and tried to do as he said. Diablo calmed almost immediately and Dean gave a wicked grin.

"See? You can do it."

I hated him. Even if he was the best-looking thing ever to have crossed my path (literally!) – I still hated him.

CHAPTER TWO

I WILL ADMIT I HATED him less and less as we gradually made our way home. When he wasn't nagging or insulting me about my riding, or being paranoid about his supposedly terrible reputation, he was – well – great. Funny and interesting, unexpectedly sensitive, and altogether rather nice.

Before I knew it we were approaching the tall wrought-iron gates of my house. Diablo, belying his name (it's another word for Devil), had been an angel, partly due to having shaken off his excess energy on that dreadful gallop, partly to the obviously soothing presence of Dean, and just a little part to my new, improved approach to riding him.

"He's enjoying it, too," Dean eyed the handsome horse with approval. "As soon as you unwound and stopped fighting him he started relaxing. He's a great fella, all he needs is a bit of help to show it."

I patted the glossy black neck. "I fell in love with him the minute I saw him. I'd never seen anything so beautiful."

"And so Daddy bought him for you," Dean said drily. "Easy life, isn't it Stacey?"

We'd been getting on so well I didn't want to start fighting now.

"We're here." I changed the subject, stating the obvious. "You're really kind to have walked all this way with me Dean."

"No problem. Jack has to have his exercise. See you, then."

"Oh, but you'll come in, won't you?" I'd cleaned up my face a bit but I wanted to show him how good I could look with a proper repair job.

"No, I won't, thanks." He'd already started walking away, Jack trotting obediently at his side.

"Bye," I called, feeling strangely deflated.

"Goodbye." He didn't turn his head. "Oh, and Stacey – get yourself a proper hat, won't you?"

"Yes Dean," I said meekly and watched him till he was out of sight.

I sighed then and pressed the code into the electronic panel that works our gates. They opened smoothly and I plodded up the long curving drive, Diablo seeming just as dejected as I was at being left on the doorstep, so to speak. All hell let loose when we finally wandered into the stable yard. My mother, who happened to be pottering around in the garden nearby, saw the stiff and cautious way I dismounted, then spotted my lacerated and still bloodsmeared face and hands. It took ages to calm her down and convince her I hadn't had a major accident or suffered any serious injury. She wanted me to go straight indoors and lie down but I told her I had to sort out Diablo first.

"You can't!" She was still shrieking a bit. "You're limping quite badly. Just put the horse in his field and leave him. I said he was dangerous, Stacey."

"No he's not." I began scraping at the dried sweat that clung to Diablo's sleek coat. "And my leg's only bruised."

"Here's your father," she said with evident relief. "Don, come and see to Stacey. She's had a terrible fall."

My dad's worried, kindly face appeared immediately.

"What happened? Are you hurt? I said I didn't like you going out alone, Stacey. Diablo's a far cry from Dolly and I'm not convinced he's safe."

Dolly was my pony mare, a 13.2 sweetie-pie

who was the original calm, bombproof equine schoolteacher. I'd been ambling about on her every school holiday for years without suffering anything worse than a bruised toe where she trod on me. Diablo, horse of my dreams as he was, was proving to be a total contrast in almost every way, and was, if I'm honest, one heck of a shock.

"I promise you, Dad, he's all right." I made a huge effort and added "It's me. I don't really know how to handle him. Maybe I could have lessons?"

His face lit up at once. "Of course, of course. Lessons are a marvellous idea. I'll book some straight away."

"I think you should change the horse, anyway." My mother made him sound like a library book. She's really very nice, but so unhorsey, so un-animally, I sometimes wonder where I get my own passion from.

"I don't want another horse. I want Diablo," I said firmly. "I love him but I don't ride him well."

"Who's been talking to you?" Dad asked shrewdly. "You've always vetoed the idea of taking lessons, said you'd picked up all you needed to know riding Dolly."

"Mm." I thought of the scorn in Dean's eyes. "Well, I was wrong. This – this boy helped me today and he pointed out a few things."

"Good for him." Dad's face was now beaming in relief. "You should have brought him in so I could thank him. Who is he?"

"Dean someone." I stopped brushing for a moment to see if the name had any effect.

Dad shook his head. "Don't know him. Mind you, we've hardly met anyone yet have we? Maybe Dean could recommend a good riding teacher."

"And a groom." Mum was still looking anxious. "Stacey shouldn't have to spend all this time cleaning up and – and mucking out and so on. If we had a groom she could just leave the horse and come indoors."

"I wouldn't want to." I laughed at her worried expression. "It's part of the fun. Dolly's always lived out, but Diablo has to come in at night and now we've got this great stableyard I really enjoy doing all the chores."

"I don't understand it." She looked at her beautifully manicured nails. "I love the house but I'm jolly glad we employ a cleaner."

"You leave Stacey alone." Dad's eyes were twinkling. "If she wants to look after the old devil horse, all credit to her. D'you want a hand with anything?"

"No thanks." I put Diablo's smart new head-collar on. "I'll let him have an hour or so in the paddock with Dolly and Griswald before I do his evening feed and everything."

Griswald's a grumpy old cob I saw being

brutally whipped on a beach two years ago. He's quite elderly and couldn't manage the work they were trying to make him do, so I got Dad to buy him as company for Dolly. You'd think he'd have become sweet natured through sheer gratitude wouldn't you, but he hasn't. He still gives you the odd nip when you pick his feet out and he knocked the vet right over when he had his last flu jab. Dolly likes him though, and even new boy Diablo has taken to grazing companionably close to the old bear. I finished brushing and hobbled over to fetch the lightweight rug I'd started using now the cooler autumn weather was here. Dad's grin of amusement at what he called my "molly-coddling" of the horses changed to a look of concern.

"You really are limping. I thought your mother was just fussing."

"It's nothing much." I was glad now I hadn't been allowed to do the "spoilt brat" act and Diablo and I had made our own way home. "I landed in some bushes so they broke my fall."

"How exactly did you come to fall?" Dad was still looking worried. "It wasn't this Dean's fault was it? I know when young lads start showing off they can be pretty irresponsible."

"It wasn't like that at all." I pushed down a surge of irritation. "Thanks to Dean neither the horse or I came to any harm. He was quite a hero actually."

"He certainly seems to have made an impact. I wish I'd met him, anyone who can make you change your stubborn little mind about riding lessons gets my vote any time."

"I'm not stubborn." Everyone seemed to be getting at me today." Open the door for me, Dad."

He stood back as I walked, trying not to limp too badly, out into the yard. The other horses were in the larger of the winter fields which ran alongside the yard wall and they whinnied a greeting as we approached. Diablo called back eagerly, his neck arched in a beautiful, classic curve. As soon as I removed the headcollar he was off, cantering freely to join his friends, without a backward glance or thought for me. I was beginning to feel a little sorry for myself, what with my horse's cavalier treatment and the barrage of criticism I'd suffered from Dean and even my soft, adoring old dad.

Once indoors I peeled off my jodhpurs and examined the sore leg. It was already turning an interesting colour in several places, so I prodded myself gingerly to make sure it was only bruising. The prodding made me wince but I could bend everything that should bend and there was only slight swelling so it was obvious I'd done nothing major. Turning my attention to my face proved more harrowing. Honestly, I looked like something out of a low budget vampire film. The scratches were all superficial but I'd smeared the blood around quite freely and added a tasteful coating of dirt from my grimy hands. My eyelashes were caked with grey dust giving me a curiously washed-out and docile look and my hair, which I'd fondly imagined to be merely romantically wind tousled, was speckled with clay of an elderly whitish shade.

No wonder Dean hadn't been any more impressed with my appearance than he'd been with my riding prowess. I sighed and tried not to think about his own good-looking face with its strong classical features, those fabulous clear grey eyes and the grin that – I shook myself severely and stepped into the shower. I felt better after a good soaping and hair wash, though my leg was still uncomfortable. I hobbled through Diablo's evening routine of rug changing and feeding, giving him one last forgiving kiss before limping back to the house.

Dolly and Griswald got a nice little feed too, though they really don't need it being retired from work with all our lovely grass to eat. They've always lived out, with a good, stout field shelter they hardly ever use except on hot days, but Diablo has different breeding altogether, with fine skin and a much thinner coat.

I've always liked the stable chores side of being

involved with horses and learnt a lot about care and management when I first got Dolly. We bought her from a very prestigious equitation centre which was near the house where we used to live in Surrey. I'd done the usual pester pester pester routine until my dad had agreed I could go riding, and from the very first moment I sat on Dolly's back I knew this was something I really wanted to do. My parents are lovely I know, though there are days when they drive me mad, but they've always been a bit too indulgent and I've always been a lot too headstrong. The result was that instead of booking me in for six months' lessons at the riding school, Dad listened to my pleading, got out his cheque book, and bought Dolly outright there and then.

We had nowhere to keep her so she stayed as a resident at the centre, and I could see her whenever I wanted. I was already at boarding school so in fact it wasn't anywhere near the every day arrangement that I'd have liked, but every holiday and a lot of weekends were spent with her.

Unfortunately, though I adored following Jessop, the head groom, around and learning the ropes about grooming, feeding, bandaging, plaiting and all the rest of it, my few experiences in the manege for riding lessons were a total disaster.

I hated the tutor, she was bossy and snobbish and she used expressions my ten year old never-been-horsey-before brain just hadn't heard of, like changing diagonals and maintaining contact and impulsion. Apparently I did them all wrong and I will admit, not being the greatest person at taking criticism, I spent most of the lessons in a deaf, dumb and blind towering sulk.

My mum said later that the teacher was very hard on me because she didn't like the fact we'd bought Dolly, who was just the most brilliant pony any school could have. Whatever the reason, instructor and pupil clashed very badly indeed and once I could more or less do rising trot I abandoned the manege completely and simply took Dolly out for hacks across the common on my own. Not to be recommended of course, and Jessop and most of the other staff told me so, but I dug my heels in and just refused ever to go back and be taught anything at all about riding. A year or so later we moved to the Midlands where Dad was opening some new factories and this time we had an old farmhouse with six acres of land, so Dolly lived with us and I rode just as I liked.

The little mare was so good, totally patient and honest in everything she did, and I could see now that it was to her credit, not mine, that I never got hurt or even vaguely frightened in all the years that I'd been riding her. And then – another move to the lovely manor house in Dorset and my sighting of Diablo. He really is the most beautiful horse you've ever seen, a true, glowing black, perfect conformation, handsome head, flowing mane and tail – in fact pure Hollywood. He also happens to have a kind disposition and though it's not usually an attribute talked about in horses, a great sense of fun. He's young and has been very well broken and schooled, but after just a few weeks of my less than proficient riding he was getting out of hand.

I'd had a couple of scares before today's out of control gallop and although I was sure Diablo was only having his idea of a good time, being run away with is a frightening, horrible feeling and I never wanted to experience it again.

Dean had quickly summed up my fear. Despite the attempts at joke cracking I'd been completely unnerved, and I'm sure if he hadn't made me get back aboard there and then I just wouldn't have been able to ride Diablo ever again. I screwed up my face in self disgust. What a mess I'd made of riding the wonderful horse so far, and a complete and utter mess was how Dean must think of me.

"If he thinks of me at all." I stared at my reflection in my dressing-table mirror and poked out my tongue. "I wonder if it's worth trying to contact him and ask if he can recommend a riding instructor?"

My face, once cleaned up, didn't look too bad, mostly light scratches with one deep gouge across my forehead but my hair hid most of that. If I wore my new boots and the brilliant jacket mum got me last week, I could make quite an impression when I went to look for Dean.

Early the next morning I went to find Mrs Locke, the local lady who helps us in the house.

"Morning, Stacey" she greeted me with her lovely Dorset burr. "Been down to the stables already have you?"

"Mmm," I smiled back. "Diablo likes his breakfast at seven and after he'd finished I put him out in the field with the others."

"Good for you." She peered closely at my face. "That's a nasty cut. Have you come off again?"

I didn't like the "again". How come everyone seemed to know how many times I'd hit the floor during the last few weeks?

"It's nothing." I trotted out my standard reply. "It happened on the far side of the downs actually and while I was there I met someone from round here. Er – Mrs Locke, I was going to ask if you knew him." I paused. "His name's Dean. I don't know his surname – "

"And you don't want to." She picked up a cushion and plumped it with what I thought was unnecessary violence. "I wondered how long it would be before Dean spotted you. You keep away from him, Stacey. Your mum and dad won't want his type hanging round here. He's nothing but trouble that one, you just mark my words."

CHAPTER THREE

I SPENT THE NEXT TEN MINUTES trying to persuade her to be more specific. Just why was Dean such bad news, what exactly had he done I wanted to know? Mrs Locke would only mutter darkly about "steering clear" and Dean being "not my sort" and having "ideas above his station", whatever that might be. In the end I gave up in exasperation and stomped off to make myself some breakfast.

I was on my second lot of toast by the time Dad came downstairs and waved a slice around while I told him what Mrs Locke had said.

"Calm down, Stacey," he said, quite sharply for him. "You're showering me in marmalade. What exactly did she say he'd done?"

"That's just it!" I slammed the toast down. "She didn't. It was all implication and innuendo and – and rubbish. Trying to make me stay away from him! Well, tough, because I'm going out today to find him."

"You most certainly are not." I'd never heard my dad sound like that. "Stop working yourself into a tantrum and behave yourself. Until we know just what the problem is, you are to do exactly what Mrs Locke said and keep out of his way."

"What?" I stared at him open mouthed. "But that's totally unfair. He probably hasn't done anything worse than scrump a few apples from her garden."

"If that proves to be the case then you can certainly contact him again. But not, I repeat, Stacey, not till I've satisfied myself this Dean is all right."

I can't tell you how poleaxed I felt. This was my dad, my soft, indulgent, ever kindly dad laying down the law in a way I'd never heard before.

"But you said." I knew I sounded like a petulant three year old. "You said I should ask Dean to recommend a riding instructor."

"That was before I knew there might be a problem with the boy." He looked at me in his usual tender way. "I think his suggestion you get lessons was an excellent one and I'm sure you're right and he's perfectly OK – but, and this is a big BUT, Stacey, you are not to see Dean until I've found out more about him."

I could see it was pointless to argue. I'd never, now I came to think of it, actually argued with Dad before. Sometimes when I wanted something I'd had to wheedle a bit, just keep on and on till he gave in, but on those occasions he'd only ever stalled me with a gentle "we'll see" or "I expect so", not, as in this case, a heavy and most definite NO.

I left the toast and shuffled back to my room feeling slightly strange. I could, I suppose, have simply ignored what he'd said and got dressed up as planned to go looking for Dean. Oddly enough, though I prided myself on defying authority in the shape of snooty riding instructors and over-bossy teachers at school, I didn't really want to disobey my dad. He made so few rules I thought I owed it to him to respect this one and I trusted him enough to realise he'd keep his promise if Dean's bad reputation turned out to be fiction.

I sat down and looked at the smart jacket and boots I'd put ready to wear, then with a sigh, put them back in the cupboard. I'd dressed hurriedly at half-past six in old jods and a huge, slightly tatty sweater that's my favourite. As I now wouldn't be going anywhere there didn't seem much point in changing so I ambled back downstairs and shrugged myself into my coat and wellies.

I'd already skipped Diablo's stable out and thrown his bed up but I decided a proper scrub up and some tack cleaning wouldn't go amiss. I wasn't, if I'm honest, that mad keen to go riding. My leg was still stiff and the thought of wrestling with the exuberant black horse all on my own wasn't that appealing. The sooner I could get these lessons organised the better.

Still, today wasn't going to be the day for that, so I might just as well spend it getting everything in the yard in good order. I worked most of the morning, taking ages checking the three horses over (and giving them a lot of cuddles). Dolly and Diablo loved every minute, picking up their feet beautifully and nuzzling my hair when I oiled their hooves, and even Griswald only nipped me once, which is as near as he gets to being affectionate. When I'd done everything I could think of, I turned them all out again and watched them trot joyously back into their beloved field.

Dolly and Diablo lay down in almost the same spot and enjoyed a squirmy, leg waving roll, while the old cob was satisfied with rubbing his back end firmly against a fence post to relieve an itch.

I sat on a rail laughing my head off as I watched them. Diablo turned to look at me, his handsome head powdered clownishly with dust and a gleam of shared amusement in his eyes. Well that's what I thought anyway. He soon lost interest in me though, and within minutes all three were cropping grass busily. I slid off the fence and wondered what to do next. The trouble with moving, even to a great place like Deepdene, was that I didn't have any friends around. I'd talked my parents out of sending me back to boarding school and hadn't really decided what college course to take, so I was at a loose end.

I ran my hand disconsolately over the stout post and rail fence we'd had put in and realised I hadn't checked the whole paddock. It's a fairly big field, stretching away to the perimeter of our land, which borders the grounds of Hazelgrove House, our nearest neighbour. I pushed my hair out of my eyes with a grimy hand, wishing I'd tied it out of the way, and started plodding along the line of fencing, checking for any signs of damage, any gaps that might prove a problem.

The far end, which was the shared border between us and Hazelgrove, was thickly planted with blackthorn and it took longer to make sure that each post was firmly in place. I was stooping to push aside some bramble when I heard voices, loud, angry voices from behind the thick screen of hedgerow.

"And I'm telling you he's snooping." A man's voice, with a slight London accent and a lot of fury.

"I'm sure you're wrong Mr – er – " The second man sounded placatory, his local burr strong. "He's a good, hard-working lad. Been with us a while now and no trouble at all. It's his lunch break, he was just having a look round I expect."

I started to move off, feeling inexplicably guilty at eavesdropping on a row, even though it was quite unintentional.

"Is that so?" London positively snarled. "Always takes a look round with a camera does he?"

I was intrigued, but was still walking away – honestly! – when the quieter, Dorset voice stopped me in my tracks.

"Is that true Dean? Is that your camera the gentleman's got?"

Dean! The name was enough to turn me straight round and when I heard his voice I felt the hairs on the back of my neck start to tingle.

"Yes." He sounded different, less sure of himself than yesterday. "But I was only taking pictures of a horse for my painting, Mr Lovall, that's all."

"Ah, that's what it is then. He paints, you see." I could imagine the kind, country face as he explained to Mr Angry. "I've seen some of his stuff. Quite a talent, especially when it comes to horses. You should have asked permission before you took photos though, Dean."

"Paintings, my foot," only Mr Angry didn't say foot. "He's snooping. He's a nasty piece of work and my employer doesn't want him on the premises, Lovall. You get rid of him now or you lose the contract."

"Oh now, now, that's a bit harsh, surely. Dean won't do it again, will you my lad?"

"I can't." The boy sounded sullen and defeated. "He's broken my camera."

"No need for that, surely." Mr Lovall was quite shocked, I could hear it in his voice. "He's only a lad Mr – er – "

"Your lad here broke it himself when he attacked me." The other man had calmed down but there was a vicious edge to his words.

"Attacked you?" Now Mr Lovall really was shocked, and Dean gave a harsh laugh.

"I simply took the camera from him and he went for me like a madman. I could prosecute, you know, Lovall. We could call the police now if you're not getting shot of the young trouble-maker."

"You don't want the police," Mr Lovall said hurriedly. "Perhaps if he apologised? Come on now, Dean – "

"You're not listening to me, Lovall." The cocky London tone seemed more menacing now he'd stopped shouting somehow. "Dean is to go. Dean is to be sacked now, this very minute, and Dean is never, ever to set foot on this land again."

"You can't get me sacked!" There was a desperate note in the boy's voice. "It's all rubbish, Mr Lovall. I didn't attack this man – he nearly wrenched my arm off when he snatched the camera but I didn't retaliate."

"Calling me a liar now, are you?" London was oily smooth. "What's it to be then, Lovall, do we call the police or do we send this lout packing?"

"You're only a hired hand yourself" Dean burst out. "It's not up to you."

"The lad's right. I think Mr Randall should be informed what's happening."

Mr Randall was, I knew, the owner of

Hazelgrove House, though I hadn't yet met him.

"Inform away." My heart sank at the confident way London said it. "I think you'll find him in the study."

I heard Mr Lovall plodding loudly off, then the distinct sound of a scuffle.

"Come on, Dean, get walking. It's my word against yours and who d'you think's going to be believed. If you leave now Randall won't call the police. Once the law gets involved you'll have no hope, believe me."

"Let go of me!" Dean's anger and frustration were obvious. "What's this all about, why are you so scared of a few photos?"

"I think we both know what we're talking about here Dean. Now are you going to leave, or am I going to have to throw you out? If you get beaten up I'll just have to say you attacked me again and I hit you in self-defence."

I gave an involuntary squeak and the man said sharply, "What's that? Come on, I mean it, get moving, Dean. I want you out of that main gate in five minutes flat."

I heard Dean, still protesting, begin to walk away and I ran desperately along the fence trying to follow them. It was no good, they'd moved away from our border and the only thing I could think of was to sprint out to the road outside and try and meet Dean when he came out (got thrown out?) of Hazelgrove's gates. Fast running in wellies is not easy. It had been a wet autumn so far and as I squelched frantically back across the field I knew I wouldn't be in time. It took me nearly five minutes at an exhausting rapid plod to reach our drive on the far side of the field and when I got there all I could do was lean weakly against the fence, lungs bursting. My dad's Range Rover was heading towards me, returning sedately to the house. I waved my arms to flag him down and he leaned out of the window in concern.

"Stacey, what's the matter? Are you ill?"

I was so out of breath I could hardly speak but I gasped out everything I'd heard, and Dad, bless him, reacted immediately.

"Jump in." He was already spinning the car round.

"Where are we – " I was bemused.

"To get Dean. I want a word and now's as good a time as any. Quick Stacey."

My poor leg, still sore from the day before's battering, was now protesting at the treatment it was getting and I only just managed to scramble inside before the Range Rover roared off in a very unaccustomed style.

"So you definitely got the impression that this, what was he – a gamekeeper or something? – was lying to Mr Lovall?" Dad had picked up the gist of the story really well.

"Definitely," I said, still trying to breathe normally. "He more or less said so when he and Dean were alone."

"More or less." Dad frowned as he punched in the remote control to open the gates. "It's still actually Dean's word against his though isn't it?"

I struggled to remember the exact words London had used. "He said something like 'if you get hurt I'll just have to say you attacked me again'. That's an admission he made the whole thing up isn't it?"

"Not really. It's a threat certainly but he didn't say he lied about Dean going for him when he grabbed the camera. Who's got this camera now, do you know?"

"It's broken." I recalled how desperate Dean had sounded. "And I don't understand what all the fuss is about, it was only used to take pictures of some horses Dean wants to paint."

"Yes, I heard he was a painter." Dad was full of surprises lately. "Quite a talented one, apparently. Look, straight ahead, is that Dean?"

We were fast approaching the big, solid looking gates of Hazelgrove and beyond them I could see a tall figure, the autumn sun picking out the pale gleam of his hair.

"Yes." I glanced to my left, where the gates had slammed firmly shut. "What are we going to do, Dad? Take him home, or back to see Mr Randall, or what?"

"We'll see." He pulled in alongside the trudging figure and called his name. "Dean. Hang on a minute. We'd like a word."

The grey eyes flicked sideways but he didn't turn his head.

"Go to hell," he said and carried on walking.

CHAPTER FOUR

"CHARMING," I THOUGHT, but poked my head out of the window anyway and said, "It's me, Stacey. Dean, I heard everything that man said and – "

He spun round immediately, his good-looking face alight. "You heard? You can back me up that he was lying, Stacey?"

"Get in and we'll discuss it." Dad was already turning the car as Dean climbed in the back, eagerly leaning forward towards me.

"Was that you on the other side of the hedge just now then, Stacey? I thought I heard someone but that gorilla couldn't wait to hustle me off the premises – well, you heard what went on."

Dad had spun the car and was driving back towards Deepdene.

Dean looked across at him in surprise. "Aren't we going in to see Mr Randall? Now that Stacey can back me up, confirm that I wasn't snooping and I didn't attack that guy, I'm in the clear, surely? I don't want to lose this job."

We were turning towards our drive and Dad tapped in the remote control to open the gates. "It's not quite as clear cut as that, I'm afraid. The snippets of conversation Stacey overheard don't really let you off the hook."

"But...." the eager light had gone from Dean's eyes. "You caught what he said when old Lovall went off, surely?"

"Yes I did." I told him quickly just exactly what I had heard, and he slumped back in the car seat, defeat written all over him.

"He let it all out when he was frogmarching me away but I suppose we were out of earshot by then. I think he also had the feeling someone was on the other side of that hedge."

"That was me," I said, none too brightly, and he shot me a jaded look.

"Yeah, I realise that. I just wish you'd heard the whole thing. Thanks for picking me up anyway, Mr Jennings. I might just as well give up and go home, though. If Stacey can't verify my story I don't have a hope of getting Mr Randall believing me."

"But that – that thug's lies have cost you your job," I said hotly. "Mr Lovall said you were a good worker, he didn't want to sack you. AND he went off to try and persuade Randall not to make you leave."

Dean shrugged resignedly. "That thug as you call him has been working there a long time. Randall isn't going to take my word against his own employee now is he? I'm just a labourer working for the gardening contractor he's taken on. My story wouldn't count for anything even without my dad – " he stopped abruptly.

"What d'you mean?" I asked. "What's he got to do with this? And why are you a labourer anyway? Everyone says you can paint and that you've got real talent. You should be at college or something?"

His lip curled into a sneer. "Hark at Little Miss Privileged. I'm not at art school because you don't get paid for going to art school whereas you do get paid for being a labourer. Not much I grant you but enough to help my mum keep the wolf from the door."

I felt my cheeks burning with rage. "Don't call me names! We might be a bit better off than you but surely your parents can afford to let you go to college?"

"Stacey, that will do." My dad still had that air of quiet command I wasn't used to. "There's no point in making personal comments, either of you. Dean, you told Mr Lovall you were using the camera to photograph horses you wanted to paint. Is that right?"

"Yes." His voice was still sullen, but seemed to hold increasing respect when he responded to Dad. "It's my first day at Hazelgrove, you see. I've been with Mr Lovall since – well, quite a few weeks now, mowing lawns and tidying smallish gardens and so on, but he's only just included me in the team that do Mr Randall's grounds. I took my camera because I'd heard he had some nice horses."

"Right. So you worked all morning – yes? – and then during your lunch break you started taking pictures of the horses."

"That's right. We were thinning trees in a copse at the back of the house but I could see three or four horses grazing in the west paddock. I ate my sandwiches and wandered on over, didn't touch anything or go into the field, just steadied the camera on the top rail and took half a dozen shots or so. I didn't hear anyone creep up on me but suddenly there he was, grabbing my camera and shoving me hard against the fence. I moved forward to reach for it back, and he slammed it, lens first, against the post, smashing it to smithereens." His hands trembled slightly and he shook his head in disbelief. "I stopped dead in my tracks and just looked at him. Honestly, Mr Jennings, I didn't lay a finger on the man. I was just too shocked, I think."

My dad nodded slowly, his eyes never leaving the boy's face. "And then what?"

"Then he grabbed me, twisted my arm up behind my back and dragged me off to the clearing where the rest of the guys eat their lunch. There was only Mr Lovall still drinking his coffee by the time we got back and thuggo was still gibbering with rage. He concocted this story about me spying and attacking him and, well you've heard the rest."

"But why?" I'd decided to forgive him for the name calling. "Why should he be so angry at you taking a few photos? What on earth would make him want to get rid of you just for that?"

"It was an excuse." Dean lowered his eyes and his expression became shuttered. "And I expect even with you to back me up, Mr Randall would still have told my boss to sack me. They don't want me there and this is as good an excuse as any to get rid of me."

"Why?" I repeated stubbornly. "Mr Lovall said you were a good worker. Why shouldn't they want you to stay?"

"It's not me, exactly." Dean looked suddenly very vulnerable. "It's – oh you don't want to hear about it. Thanks for trying to help, Stacey. I'll get on home now. I've got some job hunting to do."

"Just a minute, Dean." We were still sitting in the car, now parked outside the front of our house, and Dad, who'd been leaning against the driver's door as he turned to watch Dean talking, straightened up and started getting out. "We're just about to have some lunch. From the sound of it you didn't have much chance to enjoy yours, so come on in and join us."

"No thanks, honestly." His expression was wary again. "I'll walk on back."

"Oh come ON, Dean," I said impatiently. "It's the least you can do to make up for the blisters I've got trying to catch up with you."

"Blisters?" He looked at me uncomprehendingly and I waggled an inelegant welly at him.

"On my feet – you try running in these! I've done more damage than Diablo did when he dumped me yesterday."

His face broke into a reluctant grin, transforming it instantly. "You've had a rough couple of days, haven't you Stacey?"

"Here we go then." Dad had obviously decided not to take no for an answer and shepherded Dean round the side of the house to the back door.

We left our mucky boots in the porch and padded into the warm kitchen.

"What'll it be then?" Dad was briskly washing his hands. "Beans on toast or a sandwich?"

"Beans please," I said. "And can I have some cheese as well? I'm starving."

"OK. Same for you Dean?"

"Just the beans please." He looked bemused I thought, and no wonder – he'd been set on, lied about, sacked and thrown out all in the space of a few minutes, and now here he was in Deepdene Manor, virtually kidnapped and being force fed!

"I hope we're not being too pushy." I felt quite guilty. "We just want to help."

"I know and I appreciate it." Dean looked

straight at me and I instantly wished I'd bothered to dress up a bit more.

I ran my hand self-consciously through my hair and he grinned again, making my heart leap gymnastically.

"Something funny?" I asked suspiciously, hoping against hope I didn't look that odd.

"No," he hesitated. "It's just – I didn't expect scruffy sweaters and baked beans in a house like this, somehow."

"How did you think we live – caviar off silver plates and tiaras worn at all times?" Dad doled out the food neatly and smiled in a friendly way as Dean sat down.

I knew he was trying to make the boy relax and feel confident enough to talk to us and I felt a surge of gratitude.

"Yeah, something like that." Dean tucked in, looking a bit more cheerful than he had when we picked him up.

When we'd finished I got up to make us all a mug of coffee and Dad leaned back in the kitchen chair and regarded Dean thoughtfully.

"You'll be looking for another gardening job then, will you? I'm inclined to agree with Stacey that it seems rather a waste of your talents. You're obviously a bright lad."

"Obviously." The shutters had come back down again and the defensive note was in his voice.

"Just ask anyone around here. They'll tell you I was lucky to get any job locally and no one will be surprised I've been given the boot."

"But it's so unfair," I burst out again. "This morning was just a manufactured excuse to get rid of you. I know you didn't do anything wrong and _ "

"Stacey, we've been through this," my dad said. "You didn't hear quite enough, certainly not enough to convince Mr Randall of Dean's innocence."

"No-o," I was reluctant to let it go. "But, OK, if you can't work at Hazelgrove, you can still stay on with Mr Lovall and help with his other contracts, surely?"

"No." His good-looking face was sullen. "The same thing will just keep happening. It was good of Mr Lovall to take me on in the first place and it's not fair to expect him to take all this aggro on my behalf."

"But why is everyone against you?" I thought of Mrs Locke's piece of vitriol. "What have you done to become known as the local villain?"

His expression darkened even more and Dad broke in swiftly. "Not all that much in fact. And what he has done has been under severe provocation. Right, Dean?"

He turned his head and met Dad's gaze levelly. "You've been talking to my old headmaster, haven't you? He's about the only person I can think of who'd give you that version. Ask anyone else in the town and they'll tell you, Dean Farraday's no good, in fact he's bad all through, just like his father."

"Why?" I was agog. "Come on, tell me, what have you done?"

He shrugged, feigning indifference. "Couple of disagreements, one or two fights. It's all got blown out of proportion, the way they talk round here. Everyone's ready to believe the worst when it comes to stories about me. I've given up caring what they think."

But he hadn't. I'm no psychologist but I could see that beneath the sullen expression and tough talk he was hurt and suffering.

"And your father?" I said it gently, and felt rather than saw the involuntary movement my own father made as if to stop me.

"In prison," he said flatly. "He's serving five years for grievous bodily harm and attempted burglary. The judge said he was a violent man and there's plenty who'll say I'm just like him."

I was very careful not to flinch or recoil, in fact I hardly showed any adverse reaction at all, but my good old dad was even better.

"Not in this house," he said firmly. "In fact we Jennings pride ourselves on making up our own minds based on what we know rather than what other folk think we should know. Isn't that right, Stacey?"

"Absolutely." I nodded, wondering who was going to put Mrs Locke right on that one.

"And" Dad continued, "we're so sure of your own qualities, Dean, that I'd like to offer you a position here at Deepdene, starting straight away."

My iron self-control wobbled like jelly and my jaw dropped in a way that must have looked pretty comical, especially as it reflected perfectly the incredulous open-mouthed look that Dean gave him.

"You're giving me a job?" he said

"You're giving him a job?" I said simultaneously (only my squeak was much higher).

"It's not much." Dad was busying himself tidying up at the sink, and if I didn't know better I'd have said he was trying to think of something quick. "Helping in the garden – even with most of the grounds turned over to grazing, there's still a lot of work. And of course there's the yard."

"You mean the stables?" Dean was brightening by the minute and I tried not to glare at my father.

"Mm." His back was turned firmly to me. "Stacey's mother was saying only yesterday that she thought we needed someone to help with the horses. And you know quite a lot in that line don't you?"

"Oh yes." The enthusiasm just shone out of

Dean's gorgeous grey eyes. "My uncle had a farm and kept a couple of hunters. I worked with them since I was so high and – well, I'd love to look after your three, Stacey. Can I take a look at the yard now? In fact I could start work straight away, couldn't I?"

He was on his way out of the door, actually pulling on his boots outside, before I managed to get my dad's attention.

"What's all this?" I hissed, as quietly as I could. "I said I didn't need any help with the horses."

He dropped his eyes guiltily. "I'm sorry." It was barely a whisper. "But I know what he's going through. He needs someone on his side, Stacey, someone to give him a chance."

I tried to look as if I was making a huge personal sacrifice. "All right," I said and started to make my way outside.

It was all happening too fast for me. Only this morning I'd been told in no uncertain terms to keep right out of the boy's way and here I was, a few hours later, about to show the notorious Dean Farraday his way round the newly created post of head groom at Deepdene.

"Come on, Stacey," the brand new head groom yelled. "I need to get a good look at the grounds before it gets dark."

I sighed and plodded after him. Apart from his fabulous eyes he wasn't my idea of an employee

45

and judging by the day before I didn't know if I'd
be able to stand his bossing, but, what the heck, it
was going to fun trying!

CHAPTER FIVE

IN FACT, COMPARED to our first meeting, there was barely a word of criticism from Dean. I think he was quite taken aback at his first sight of the stable yard and I felt so proud of its perfect, pristine condition it almost stopped me regretting my own tatty appearance.

"You do all the work yourself?" Dean surveyed the neat, scrubbed yard and tried to keep the surprise out of his voice.

"Uh huh," I replied casually. "I give Diablo his breakfast at seven then come back and turn him out in his waterproof rug before I start on the chores."

"You certainly seem to know what you're doing." He peered quite disconsolately into my tidy tack room. "I'm not at all sure your dad's right about you needing help."

I didn't want him turning the job down so I quickly said "I'm only bringing Diablo in at the moment, but later on when it gets really cold the other two will probably be in at night as well. And of course when I go to college I won't have as much time."

"Right." His expression was noncommittal and I hoped he hadn't realised Dad had virtually invented the job to "give him a chance" as he'd put it. "Can I see the horses now?"

"Sure." I walked with him to the paddock gate. "They're in the far corner, wouldn't you know it. That's where I was when I heard the row going on in Hazelgrove. I was walking round checking all the fencing."

"That's good." He shielded his eyes against the sun that hung low in the autumn sky and seemed to scan the distant hedgerow.

"What d'you think of them?" I asked and he shifted his gaze immediately to look at the horses.

"They're very nice. I've seen Diablo of course and I heard you had a couple of others more or less as companions. The cob's pretty old, isn't he?"

"That's Griswald." I gave him a brief history of the old boy and told him about Dolly and how we'd bought her too.

He seemed amused until I got to the bit about hating the riding teacher and never attending lessons.

"No wonder Diablo was able to run away with you yesterday. You need to start right from scratch, unlearn all the bad habits you've picked up and learn to ride properly."

"Here we go again," I thought but bit my lip and controlled myself. "Perhaps you could teach me then, Dean."

"I'm not qualified. There are one or two people locally you could go to. They can start you off with the basics, go on to a little simple dressage and – "

"Dressage!" I squealed as if it were a dirty word. "Oh I don't want to bother with all that. It's so boring. I wouldn't mind having some jumping lessons. Dolly hops over logs and streams with no problem but when I've tried on Diablo he just gets overexcited and muddles his legs up somehow."

Dean shook his head gravely. "You shouldn't even be thinking about jumping until you know how to go properly on the flat. And don't be so quick to dismiss dressage as boring. It certainly isn't dull and it'd be the perfect route for you and Diablo – get some calm and sense into the pair of you instead of thundering round the country totally out of control."

I opened my mouth to snarl that if I didn't want to learn boring old dressage there was no way anyone could make me, but in the light of what Dad had said I closed it again. Dean was already making his presence felt. I'd practised more restraint and self-control in the last two days than in the whole of my life so far.

"Right." Dean dragged his eyes away from the far side of the paddock and looked briskly around. "Where would your dad like me to start? On the garden presumably, seeing that you have the stable side so well looked after."

I racked my brains. "Um – there's always muck collecting in this paddock of course, but you'll have to ask Dad about the gardening."

"Show me where everything's kept then." He was no slouch that was for sure. I showed him where the barrow and dung heap were and rather reluctantly left him. He called, "I'll start trimming that hedge round the rose garden when I've finished here unless Mr Jennings wants me to do anything else."

"OK." I'd decided to nip off and do something about my appearance. "I'll tell him."

I ran indoors and rushed up to my room to check how I looked. "Ghastly!" I told my reflection. "You look like a scarecrow. Straw in your hair and dirt on your face and this old sweater makes you look about twelve years old. What shall I WEAR?"

I cleaned myself up first then had a good rummage in my wardrobe. The smart coat and boots were far too dressed up to wear around the house but I was determined Dean would see me looking at least presentable. In the end I picked out some better fitting jeans and a shirt that brought out the colour in my eyes. They're very blue, and nicer people than Dean have commented on them. I fiddled about quite a lot with my hair as well and even put some concealing stuff over the worst of the scratches on my face.

Sauntering casually back downstairs I was disconcerted when my dad gave me a mock wolf whistle and said, "Where are you off to looking so gorgeous?"

"I don't look gorgeous," I said indignantly and messed my hair up a bit to show how unconcerned I was. "I've just – um cleaned off some of the muck from this morning."

"Right," he agreed, perfectly straight faced. "If you're not going anywhere special then perhaps you'd like to take young Dean a mug of coffee? He's been working nonstop – he's done nearly half the hedge already."

"Oh all right." I took the cup and made my way to the rose garden.

Dean had certainly been busy. Half the shaggy, overgrown yew hedge was now neatly shorn and he was vigorously sweeping the clippings into a tidy pile.

"Tea break," I called. "Well it's coffee actually."

"Great, thanks." He sat down on a bench and pulled his rucksack from underneath it. "Are you joining me?"

"I thought I might." I put my own cup on the ground and, feeling slightly shy, sat at the other end of the bench. I thought he'd been reaching in the rucksack for more sandwiches or something but to my surprise he brought out a sketch pad and pencil. For one wild moment I thought he wanted to draw ME and went all hot and cold with embarrassed excitement. As soon as he began

51

making a few rapid strokes with the pencil it was obvious he was drawing something from memory and I sank back, half relieved. I risked a sly peek and saw the rather lovely outline of a horse.

"Who is it?" I asked. "Diablo? It's too fine to be either of the other two – oh what's that?"

Dean had quickly sketched in the outline of markings on the head, neck and flanks of the horse. "That's not my boy, he's all black."

"It's just a skewbald I saw this morning. He – took my eye and I'd like to paint him."

"Oh, he was one of those you saw in Hazelgrove was he – the ones you took the photographs of? Honestly Dean, if that great ape hadn't smashed up your camera like that you'd have been able to copy the markings from the photo wouldn't you?"

"Er – yes." He seemed to want to change the subject. "You look different Stacey. What have you done?"

I felt immediately self-conscious and defensive. "Nothing. Well, I cleaned off this morning's dirt I suppose."

"And you've got make-up on now." He sounded amused.

"No I haven't. It's – it's just a sort of ointment for the scratches."

"Let me see." His long, work roughened fingers were surprisingly gentle. "That's quite a nasty one on your forehead. Lucky you have all this mass of hair to hide it."

I shook my curly locks, hoping he liked it. "It's a mess isn't it?"

"The hair or the scratches?" He laughed at my outraged face. "Just kidding. You look really nice. In fact, you are nice, not at all what I thought you'd be like."

I swallowed and decided to take it as a compliment. "Thanks. Though why you should have decided otherwise without ever meeting me – "

"It's the Rich Bitch thing," he said quite seriously. "Everyone knows your dad's got loads of money and seems to like spending it on you. And when I met you yesterday the first impression you gave was very much the spoilt brat."

"And now?" I was trying to sound casual, as if his opinion of me didn't matter, but I knew deep down that it mattered an awful lot.

"You work hard and you look after your horses really well. I'm impressed, though I'll be even more so if you stick to the riding lessons."

I pulled a face. "It all depends on the tutor. I hate bossy sorts or the kind who look down on you if you don't know the correct expressions. I can't be bothered to learn all that."

"Here we go." Dean stood up abruptly and handed me his empty mug. "You've got to drop that attitude, Stacey. You owe it to poor old Diablo if nothing else. Learn to ride properly, and that includes learning the right names for everything. You bothered to learn stable management and horse care thoroughly so why not equitation?"

I looked up at him. The grey eyes that seemed to change shade with every mood, were deep and warm and looking directly into mine. I really wanted to please him, to say nothing that would put that cold glint of steel in his gaze.

I flashed my best smile and said, "I'm going to try, I promise."

The grin he gave me sent my pulse rate up several notches and I nearly floated back indoors. Fired up with enthusiasm I told Dad to book me in wherever he'd decided was the best establishment for riding lessons. I was slightly taken aback when he told me less than an hour later that I was due to start the very next day!

"The girl who took the call sounds nice and says the teacher's highly qualified." He looked really happy at the thought. "And I said we'd box Diablo over until you've got him under control a bit more. It's only a couple of miles away – "

"Oh terrific!" I said with heavy sarcasm. "That'll create a really good first impression won't it. Everyone will be laughing at this new pupil who's too scared to even ride her horse two miles down the road."

"It's not a question of your being scared, I know that." Dad was wearing his usual totally-mystified-at-Stacey expression. "Diablo threw you quite badly and I don't want it happening again so – "

"He didn't throw me, I fell off," I interrupted him again. "And that was only because I'd let him gallop away with me. There won't be any chance of that happening on a two mile road trip. And he's brilliant in traffic, you know that."

Dad shrugged helplessly. "OK, if you say so. Maybe Dean could walk with you just to make sure?"

"Dad!" I almost shrieked. "That would be even worse than arriving in a horsebox. Just leave me to it will you?"

"All right." He was back to being my compliant, indulgent Dad again. "But we must do one thing before the lesson. Dean says you need a proper hat."

I felt the mulish look start to settle on my face and tried hard to replace it with a grateful smile.

"It'll probably be the first thing the tutor mentions. Maybe we should postpone the lesson till we can buy one."

"No need. They've got a full range of BHS approved hats at Fletchers Saddlery. I phoned just now and they're open till five thirty. Let's go, shall we?" I could hardly refuse could I, and we drove off more or less straight away.

When we got back there was no sign of Dean

and I thought he must have gone for the day. It was already starting to get dark so I changed back into my scruffy stuff and went out to the paddock to bring Diablo in. All three horses had gone back to the far corner and although I called their names they'd all decided to go deaf and totally ignore me. I plodded over, thinking rather glumly about the next day's riding lesson and wondering whether I'd get away with saying my leg hurt too much to do it. The autumn dusk was drawing in very quickly and the thick tangle of hedgerow on the perimeter of the field was already an inky black mass. The horses still had their backs to me and I approached Diablo quietly, talking softly so as not to alarm him. He whickered with pleasure and dropped his velvet nose into my palm. I stroked his ears and started telling him how handsome and wonderful he looked when he spooked suddenly and shot forward, nearly knocking me flying.

"Sorry, that was my fault." I hadn't seen the dark shape emerge from the line of trees and gave an involuntary squeak.

"Dean! I thought you'd gone home. Where have you been?" It was a stupid question. There was only one place he could have come from – the very place he'd been thrown out of earlier that day and told never, ever to step foot in again – the grounds of Hazelgrove House.

CHAPTER SIX

"I JUST THOUGHT I'D SEE if there was any chance my camera had been chucked down on the other side of your fence." He busied himself pulling a burr or two from Dolly's tail and didn't look at me.

"Bit of a dangerous thing to do," I said, buckling on Diablo's headcollar, "seeing how violent things got this afternoon."

"I wasn't up to anything if that's what you think." He started striding angrily away. "I just wanted a look but I didn't trespass, there's no getting through that tangle of hedge."

"Not here you can't." I was nearly running to keep up with him. "Slow down a bit, it's no good getting in a temper with me."

"Sorry." He turned and tried to smile. "I seem to be on a pretty short fuse at the moment, thinking everyone's having a go at me."

"I'm not surprised." My heart went out to him. "Look, if a camera's so important you can always borrow mine."

"No it's OK, thanks. I was hoping if I found mine there'd be a chance of salvaging the film."

I thought it odd a few random shots of a group of horses should be that important but I was learning to watch what I said. Instead I changed

57

the subject by telling him about the riding lesson Dad had booked.

"I know the place," he said. "It's got a good name, bit high and mighty for the likes of me but you'll be all right."

"I don't fancy it much." I was still gloomy at the thought. "But I'll give it a go," I added hurriedly, seeing he was about to nag.

I went on to tell him about the new hat and Dad's comments about boxing Diablo the two miles to the riding school.

"Not a bad idea." Dean was obviously not in the least bothered about upsetting me with the things he said. "At least it'd mean the rest of the world would be safe from you two."

"Thanks a lot," I retorted huffily. "I'm perfectly capable of riding my horse a couple of miles without endangering anyone."

When it came to setting off the next morning I didn't feel anywhere near as confident however. My leg was stiff still, and Diablo, after his lazy day off, seemed more manic than ever, dancing about as I tried to climb aboard, then jig-jogging and snatching at the bit when we moved out of the yard. I was tired out before we even reached the end of our drive and although the black horse was, as usual, bombproof where traffic was concerned, he continued to break into the irritating jog and throw his head around at intervals the whole way there. I realise now I was particularly tensed up and did nothing to help him relax, but the fact was our continual battle with each other meant there was just no way that lesson was ever going to be a success. I got back home an hour and a half later, red faced and near to tears, with a jittery, frustrated Diablo who'd sweated enough to make Dean think we'd been galloping flat out again.

"Whoa, steady now." His voice, when he spoke to the horse, was gentle and soothing, but the look he shot me was pure venom. "What's he doing in this state? Have you been charging round the downs again instead of going to your lesson Stacey?"

I slid thankfully off the still dancing horse and glared at both of them resentfully. "No I have not. You saw what he was like when I left, well he just got worse. And the horrible woman at the riding centre said I was doing everything wrong and I couldn't do the stuff she wanted to put it right and Diablo tried to run out of the schooling ring and when I stopped him she said "No wonder the poor horse is going so badly for you, you just jabbed him in the mouth again." And I said "Well I don't know how to stop him" and she looked cross and said "I was told you were quite experienced and you're obviously not and the horse is not suitable for you" and – and I HATE HER."

"Oh, very adult." Dean was still intent on

calming Diablo and didn't so much as glance at me. "And now I suppose you're going to stamp your little foot and get Daddy to buy you a nice new horse because this one's no good are you?"

"You just don't get it do you?" I yelled and yanked my smart new hat off in a fury. "Of course I don't want another horse, I want to be able to ride Diablo. Only everyone's so busy telling me I'm rubbish nobody will help me do it. It's no good nagging me to go back and try again because I won't go to that woman again, not ever."

Dad had come hurrying along and was just in time to catch the last phrase. A worried frown creased his forehead and he put his arm round me and spoke in the same kind of soothing voice Dean was using on the horse.

"Now Stacey, don't get yourself so worked up. I'm sure the teacher wasn't that bad – "

I twisted away angrily. "She was. She said I wasn't competent enough to ride a young horse like Diablo but I won't give him up Dad, I love him and I won't."

He patted my back tentatively and murmured something about it perhaps being the horse's fault.

Now it was Dean's turn to bristle. "I don't think there's much wrong with Diablo, Mr Jennings. He's been well broken and properly schooled on but he's getting all the wrong signals from Stacey and it's confusing and upsetting him."

"Oh go on, now you start on me." The tears were threatening to erupt at any minute. "You seem to know so much about riding Diablo, let's see you get some sense out of him."

"OK." To my great surprise he took the hat out of my hands and led the horse towards the smaller, empty paddock. "It may take a while because he's so wound up, but I'll see if I can at least get him on the bit and walking out properly."

He swung easily into the saddle and adjusted the stirrup leathers. Dad and I stood at the gate and watched as he quietly rode the black horse in a large circle. At first Diablo jogged and pulled but gradually he calmed and after only a few minutes I could see the difference. He almost seemed to change shape as his neck curved gently from withers to poll and you could see his back and loins had relaxed and become more supple. He dropped his nose to accept the bit and his jaw was quiet, without the tension that had made him pull and snatch when I was riding him. Dean asked for trot, then when they were going forward looking nicely balanced and springy, Diablo struck off beautifully into a smooth, rhythmic canter. I could only look on enviously, my eyes worshipping the perfect picture the two of them made. Dean brought the horse back to walk and came over to join us. He dismounted expertly and silently handed me the reins. I couldn't help it, I just buried my face in Diablo's sweet-smelling neck and howled like a three year old.

"It IS my fault. If I could ride like that we'd be all right wouldn't we, Diablo?"

Dad patted me kindly again and said in his most persuasive tones, "Dean, you really seem to know what you're doing. Couldn't you teach Stacey?"

"Mr Jennings, I'm not qualified. And anyway I just don't have the temperament. I'm pretty short-tempered, patience certainly isn't my strong point and Stacey's going to need a lot of that."

"I'm going to need a miracle that's what." I was still crying, so upset I didn't even care what I looked like.

"No you're not." I thought Dean was going to pat me too but he didn't. "You've got the most important thing – you want to learn. It's just finding the right person to teach you."

"Where did you go?" I hiccuped and blew my nose in unlovely fashion.

"It was someone my uncle knew," he said slowly. "She used to school his horses, came to his farm to do it and he got her to give me lessons. She doesn't work at a riding centre or anything though so I don't think you'll get her."

"We could try." I looked at my Dad for confirmation and he nodded immediately. "Is she nice, Dean?"

I thought she must be to have put up with his

grumpiness and felt hopeful that this person might be the answer.

"She's a bit mad actually." He smiled at the thought. "Quite old and eccentric but yes, she's nice if she knows you're working hard."

"She sounds perfect. I'll give her a ring, I'm sure if I offer her enough she'll agree to come here and teach Stacey."

I nodded enthusiastically and Dean sighed, obviously making an effort to control his volatile temper. "I think you'll find it's not simply a question of money. Miss Crabtree, that's her name, only works for people she likes. I was lucky, she liked my uncle and you'll probably be surprised she liked me too. She was good to me when he died."

I hadn't realised the uncle Dean frequently mentioned was dead. I felt a flood of sympathy. No wonder he was defensive and quick tempered, he'd had so much tragedy in his life. I thought about my own pampered, cosseted existence and felt ashamed.

"I don't suppose you'd be kind enough to put in a word for me with Miss Crabtree?" I asked him humbly. "You said yourself I really want to learn and I promise I'd work as hard as she could possibly want."

He hesitated. "I haven't seen her much since my dad – since all the bother. She'll be angry I've got myself a reputation for trouble."

"I don't think so," Dad said quietly. "From what you said Miss Crabtree is a bit of an original. She's also a lady of integrity I think and she'll have recognised a like-minded person in you, Dean."

The boy flushed almost painfully. "Thanks Mr Jennings." He spoke gruffly. "I'll go round and see her tonight."

"Great!" Things were looking up and I hugged Diablo lovingly. "Don't worry black horse, help is on its way! Miss Crabtree will make a rider out of me and maybe we can start really enjoying each other."

I scraped the worst of the sweat off him and put him back in the field. Dean and my dad were deep in conversation when I got back to the yard.

"We're talking about putting in a sand school for these lessons of yours." Dad was still fired up with enthusiasm. "Dean says Miss Crabtree only ever used a roped off section of a field, but I think a proper schooling ring would be far better."

I saw Dean lift his shoulders slightly. "I wouldn't go to any expense till Miss C has agreed to teach Stacey, Mr Jennings".

"Well if she doesn't we're going to have to get someone and the school will come in useful for Stacey to practise won't it. We'll have it properly fenced and she'll be much safer for one thing."

I felt a familiar surge of irritation. "I wish you'd

stop talking as though I'm a perpetual health hazard when I'm riding," I snapped. "But sure, a sand school would be nice. We could buy some jumps too, Dad. They had some really smart ones at Fletchers."

"THAT will definitely come later." Dean's eyebrows were nearly in his hair. I suppose we were giving him an example of the money-spending-on-spoilt-brat he kept talking about. I tossed my hair to show I didn't care what he thought.

"Look, I'll get a couple of local chaps to give you a quote." He'd turned away from me. "I can always help with the labouring, that'll cut costs a bit."

"Fine, fine." Dad was rubbing his hands together with glee. "Come and help me choose the best place to site the school. You too Stacey."

It seemed we spent the rest of the day tramping around measuring things and pacing out areas. In the end a sheltered spot behind the stable block was pronounced ideal and I could see Dad couldn't wait to get started. Dean did some more work in the garden, then helped with the horses and left just as it was starting to get dark. He'd only been gone a few moments when I noticed he'd forgotten his rucksack so I picked it up and ran down the drive after him. It's a long, curving sweep of a path, and once you've rounded the front of the house there's a clear view of its entire length to the big double gates.

I jogged swiftly round the corner then stopped in surprise. I should have been able to see Dean, he should have been just ahead of me and clearly visible on his way to the gates. The drive, gleaming palely in the fading light, was completely deserted, not a sign of his tall figure anywhere. Perplexed I looked around and saw a movement to my left, across the expanse of front lawn and somewhere in the region of our perimeter fence. Curious, I ran over, just in time to see Dean push his way through the hedge, which, trimmed regularly, was much less dense than the line at the rear of the paddock. I was about to call his name, but something in the furtive way he was moving, stopped me. Instead I followed him, keeping well back in the shadows. He pushed his way through till he was padding swiftly along a path of immaculately clipped grass, bordered by ornamental shrubs. I could hear the tinkle of a fountain and knew we were now making our way through the grounds of Hazelgrove.

I caught my breath in fright, but now I didn't dare call out in case one of Mr Randall's staff was nearby. At that moment there was the sound of a car and I shrank back into the shrubbery, hoping Dean had done the same. Doors slammed and I heard loud voices, seemingly raised in argument, then the sound of footsteps, some fading towards the front door of the house, others, alarmingly, tramping in the same direction we were heading, towards the fields and paddocks at the rear. I slid forward quietly and saw Dean, his head turned towards the sound of the unseen men. I risked a rapid run towards him, grabbed his arm and virtually pulled him back towards Deepdene. He jumped violently and I put my finger to my lips and kept going. I could see the tall chimneys of our house, silhouetted against the darkening sky and had worked out more or less where we were in comparison. There was a small break in the fencing on the east side of Deepdene's front garden. When Dad trimmed the hedge a week or so earlier he'd noticed the broken paling and the gap it left in the hedge and had talked about getting it repaired. I was sure he hadn't got round to it yet and moved swiftly to the point I remembered. Luckily I was bang on target, the gap, though small, was easy to push through and we were safely back on our own ground without a sound betraying us.

I stomped a good way beyond Hazelgrove's earshot and turned to face Dean, feeling, I must say, pretty mad. "So what's the excuse this time? Thought your camera might have started walking down the drive did you?"

He shrugged his shoulders and looked mulish.

67

"Dean." I tried to keep my cool. "You know what that man said yesterday. If you so much as set foot on that land again – "

"I know, I know. I just took a quick look and saw the house was in darkness. I thought if everyone was out it would be the perfect time for a quick look round."

"But WHAT are you looking for?" I don't think I believed the story of "hoping to find the camera" the night before, let alone now.

He shook his head and wouldn't look at me.

"Oh well," I said, rather nastily I suppose, "if you want to lose the job my dad's just given you, the only job you're likely to get round here, just go ahead with your silly trespassing games."

His grey eyes flashed briefly but he still didn't speak. I wanted to scream or punch him or possibly both. Instead I turned on my heel and marched furiously back towards my house. It was only when I reached it and risked a backward glance I saw that Dean hadn't, as I'd hoped, followed me, but was slowly making his way towards the gates. And it was then I realised I still had his wretched rucksack on my shoulder. I felt inclined to hurl it into the bushes, but took a deep breath and turned round again. This time I didn't run, just walked fairly briskly, and because of the way Dean was dragging his heels I caught up with him a short way along the lane outside. I was still so mad I didn't dare speak, just thrust the rucksack at him and flounced back the way I came. It was really dark now and the lane, unlike our drive, was unlit and quite spooky. I hurried back towards Deepdene's gates, then suddenly, horribly, I bumped into someone, someone with a stranger's dark face and eyes, someone who held my arms with fingers that gripped like a vice. My nerves were already stretched to twanging point and I did an instant panic and screamed and screamed and screamed.

CHAPTER SEVEN

EVERYTHING HAPPENED SO FAST I could hardly take it in. The person I'd cannoned into let go of me immediately and at the same time came the sound of running feet. Next thing Dean came hurtling through the gloom and brought him crashing to the ground! There was a brief but frightening tussle during which I hopped up and down feeling stupid, my screams having dwindled to the occasional high-pitched squeak.

Whoever was pinned beneath Dean suddenly stopped struggling and said, "I'm trying to say I'm sorry. But the young lady actually bumped into me. All I did was try and steady her to stop her falling."

I peered into the dark face and realised it was someone virtually our own age, with dark curly hair and an expression of rueful surprise. Dean looked up at me, fair hair tousled, grey eyes alight with – what? anger? passion? Probably irritation, knowing him.

"Is that right Stacey? Did he make a grab at you or what?"

"No, he's right. I didn't see him in the dark and I walked right into him." I felt even sillier, especially when Dean straightened up and glared at me. "Why did you scream like that then? I thought you were being murdered."

"Sorry," I muttered and held out a hand to help the dark-haired lad up. "And sorry to you too. You – frightened me."

He pumped my hand up and down enthusiastically and grinned with the whitest teeth you've ever seen. "Then it's me who must apologise and I forgive your boyfriend for knocking me down."

"I am not her boyfriend," Dean growled predictably. "No wonder you scared her, what are you doing skulking round here at this time of day? There's nothing here except Deepdene where Stacey lives or – "

"I tried to call on Hazelgrove House." I knew Dean had tensed immediately. "My name's Kris Marenga by the way. Hazelgrove must be your neighbour – Stacey, was it?" The teeth flashed again, a great smile, even in the dark, and the face, though saturnine, was definitely attractive.

"Yes, it's Stacey," I could feel, positively feel Dean start to glower. "And Hazelgrove is next door to my house, you're right."

"What do you want from there?" Dean was abrupt. "Is Randall a friend of yours?"

"I wish." Kris was brushing himself down. "It's a job I'm after. I've been travelling all day, only just got here, and I suppose I should have waited till the morning. I didn't get very far with them – just rang the bell at those gates over there and a voice

71

came on the loudspeaker and told me to push off more or less."

"Why travel so far for a job here?" Dean sounded full of suspicion. "And why – "

"Look," my teeth were starting to chatter with cold. "Let's not stand out here in this freezing road. Come on back and have a coffee or something Dean, and Kris can tell you all about it."

He wasn't keen I could tell, but Kris was positively delighted. We marched back up the drive and entered our lovely warm kitchen with relief. My mum was unloading the dishwasher and she looked up in surprise. "Friends to tea ,Stacey? Oh hello Dean, it's you." You could tell by the way she spoke she wasn't as sold on Dean as my dad appeared to be. She's unfailingly polite to people though, and if Dad and I say something's OK she just smiles vaguely and goes along with it.

"And this is – er – Kris."

The dark boy leapt immediately into action, grabbing Mum's arm in the enthusiastic hand shake, and thanking her effusively for inviting him in.

"That's fine dear." She disengaged her hand gently. "Stacey will find you some tea. There are jacket potatoes and a quiche if you'd all like to help yourselves."

She floated off again and we all helped

ourselves. I'd never seen anyone eat three large jacket spuds in one go, but Kris shovelled them back as if he hadn't eaten for days.

"I haven't – well not since breakfast." He got some more quiche and another huge dollop of salad. "You're sure it's all right Stacey?"

I looked at him. He was shorter than Dean, but much stockier and the impression of a good-looking satyr still persisted even in the full light. His thick, close curling hair grew low on a broad forehead and the dark eyes, under straight black brows, seemed to sparkle with mischief. He wasn't exactly handsome, not in the classically featured way that Dean was, but the dark, wicked looks were very, very attractive.

I smiled my best bewitching smile at him and said, "Perfectly all right Kris. Now tell us all about yourself."

Dean shifted in his chair and growled something under his breath but it didn't seem to bother Kris.

"What's to tell," he said flippantly. "Usual stuff – half English half American. Since my parents died I've spent my life with Dad's family – in the circus. Now grandad's gone too, I decided it's not the life for me, touring the US, new town, new state every week. So I decided to come over to England, get a normal job and settle down."

My mouth hung open so far my chin nearly hit

the floor. "A circus? You were in a circus? What did you do?"

He shrugged. "Anything. Everything. My Dad was a high-wire artist, all his family were, but me, well I didn't have the talent or I started learning too late maybe. The family tried to teach me and I tried to learn but in the end I just did whatever was going – bit of clowning – the odd acrobatic turn – helped with the animals, you name it."

"I thought circuses with animal acts were virtually obsolete." Dean spoke rather stiffly but I could tell he was interested despite himself.

"They are in this country, hardly any of the British councils will permit animal circuses to set up so it's well and truly dying out. Different story in America though."

I rested my chin in my hand and gazed across the table at him. What a different, exotic life he'd led compared to mine. He looked back at me and ruffled my hair teasingly.

"That's quite a combination you've got, Stacey, glossy gypsy curls and dreamy blue eyes. I bet the boys at your school are queuing up to go out with you."

I smiled proudly, darting a triumphant glance in Dean's direction, then did a double take. Just how young did he think I was?

"Oh I've finished with school Kris, though I haven't done anything as exciting as you yet. So, now you've decided to give up the circus what made you choose this particular spot? What's your connection with Mr Randall?"

From the corner of my eye I noticed Dean's hands tighten to a clenched fist. Just what was the obsessive interest Randall and Hazelgrove House held for him? If he was hoping for an insight from Kris he was disappointed.

The dark head shook ruefully. "None at all. Like I said, I haven't lived in this country for a long time and I don't have any contacts at all. My mother's family must be around somewhere but she didn't stay in touch with them. All I had, literally, was Mr Randall's name and address and I picked that up from the circus."

"Someone there told you Randall would give you a job?" I didn't think that was very likely and I could tell from Dean's expression he agreed.

"No, no, it was just something I overheard. Tony Cinquetti, the guy who trains the circus horses, he was talking to his sidekick and Mr Randall's name came up. I gathered it was a wealthy bloke they were discussing so I thought Hazelgrove House was as good a place to start as any. I got to England, bought a map, wrote myself some references and here I am," he grinned winningly.

"Such a shame you didn't get a chance to show your fake credentials after all." Dean had relaxed a little I could see. "What sort of job were you going for, Kris?"

"Anything. I told you I've been a jack of all trades, can turn my hand to most things. I thought maybe butler if they still have them in big houses. But kitchen hand or garden assistant would do." He gave a sly look round the room. "Mind you, this house looks pretty impressive. I don't suppose your parents need any staff Stacey?"

I laughed at his cheek. "No, I think we're OK. We don't run to a butler and Dean's just been appointed our – um – groundsman."

"Really?" The black eyebrows raised. "So it was the truth when you said you weren't Stacey's boyfriend? The way you knocked me flying I thought it had to be true love between the two of you."

I blushed and felt all warm and girly but Dean merely scowled.

Hastily I blurted, "But if you're serious about a gardening job, Mr Lovall will have a vacancy, won't he Dean?"

The scowl deepened. "A recommendation from me won't be any good, will it, seeing the man's just sacked me."

"I don't need you to speak for me, just the guy's name and number." Kris's natural ebullience was obvious. "If there's a job going – oh and a room would be good too."

"You mean you haven't anywhere to stay?" I

squealed. He was only a year or so older than me, but I couldn't imagine being completely alone, having to be totally self-reliant with nowhere to go and no one to help.

"I've enough money to tide me over for a while," the white teeth flashed again. "And then something will turn up. It always does."

I thought briefly, crazily, about him staying at Deepdene but dismissed the idea pretty quickly. My parents are wonderfully soft and indulgent as you've seen, but I think even they would jib at agreeing to share their house with an unknown, wandering circus boy I'd known less than an hour. Dean didn't seem anxious to leave him with me either.

"I'm going back to the village now," he said gruffly. "If you want to come with me, Kris, I'll show you where you can get a B & B for the night."

Kris looked reluctant, obviously happy where he was but I said swiftly, "Good idea. You can give Kris Mr Lovall's number so he can get your old job before it's advertised."

Kris looked resigned, then the ever present smile was back and he leapt to his feet and kissed my hand with a theatrical flourish. "And we shall meet again, beautiful blue-eyed Stacey, it is written in both our stars."

Dean snorted and silently handed him his coat. As they left Dean hung back and hissed, "I wanted

77

to see Miss Crabtree on the way home but now I'm lumbered with this American romeo. Why did you have to invite him in?"

"Because I thought he knew something about Hazelgrove House." I looked at him levelly. "And since it seems you can't do a thing without thinking about the Randall setup, I thought he might be a good contact."

He grunted. "Well OK but why d'you tell him about the job with Mr Lovall?"

"For the same reason," I said calmly, proud of my logic. "If he gets the job he'll be included in the Hazelgrove contract. And there you go – instead of risking life and limb crawling round the bushes, you could get Kris to do it for you."

Dean's clear eyes held a new respect. "Just how much of what I'm doing have you worked out?"

"Very little," I admitted. "I'm hoping you'll trust me enough to tell me the whole story, but till then maybe you'll at least start believing I'm on your side."

For a moment the hard, bitter set of his features softened and he said quietly, "Thanks Stacey."

"Come on then Blondie," Kris shouted cheerfully. "Let's get going if we have to."

"Don't you dare call me Blondie." Dean's irritated voice was the last thing I heard as I closed the door and watched through the window as they were swallowed up by the inky night.

I leaned my face against the cool glass and smiled. It had been a very, very interesting day. I thought the following day would prove very flat and dull in comparison but I was proved wrong almost straight away. I'd gone back to the yard to turn Diablo out after his early morning feed and there was Dean already hard at work with the mucking out. I changed the black horse's rugs swiftly and led him out to the field.

"So, what happened with Kris?" I was agog to know. "And did you get a chance to see Miss Crabtree?"

"Oh yes." Dean's muscular arms made the job look so easy. "Yes, I saw her. I've known her since I was so high you know Stacey, and I've always been really proud she thinks well of me."

"Quite right too," I said. My dad had done some homework on the redoubtable Miss C. A force to be reckoned with and nobody's fool, was the local opinion, not someone to be taken lightly.

"Yeah, well I've always thought so." He leaned on the shovel and looked bemused. "And yet I take that – that Californian con artist in with me, simply because it'd have been too late to go back and see her otherwise, and what do you think happens?"

"Miss C agreed to take me? You talked her into coming to Deepdene?"

"Oh yes. She says you've got to do exactly what

she tells you, but as a personal favour to me she's prepared to take you on."

"So what's the problem?" He really did look put out, I thought.

"Kris. He sat there quiet as you like, only speaking when spoken to, then just as I was getting ready to leave to find him a B & B he just ups and asks Miss C if she's got a room to let. I thought she'd shrivel him up with one look but she asked him a few questions and he answered quietly, then she excused them both and off they go, then ten minutes later she comes back and says all briskly, 'Kris is in the bath. He'll be staying here a day or two. I understand Mr Lovall may have a job vacancy he'd like to apply for. Leave the phone number with me will you?'"

"That was really nice of her," I said warmly.

"Nice? NICE? Miss Crabtree isn't nice, she's – well she's great but she doesn't do nice. You just don't know her."

"So what did you do?" I was trying not to laugh at his bewilderment.

"I sort of gulped and told her the bit about Kris faking some references and she said, "that won't be necessary now, don't worry Dean. You're inclined to take on all the worries of the world and you've enough dealing with your own.""

"She's right there" I was warming by the minute to the eccentric Miss Crabtree.

"So." He gave the straw a final shake up and bent to wheel away the barrow. "She'll be here later to meet you and you can hear all about your fancy American and whether he got the job or not. There's no doubt he will of course. If he can charm Miss C into letting him stay, old Lovall will be a pushover. Just remember it's not all about him, you're supposed to convince her you really want to ride properly."

"Of course," I said with great dignity. "As long as you remember the Kris side of things is to help you with whatever mystery you're trying to sort out."

He grunted and took the barrow away, still registering disbelief at the happenings of the last few hours. I left him to it and went to check all Diablo's tack was spotless, then did the same with my riding clothes. I wanted everything to be perfect and found myself crossing fingers and toes in the hope that Miss Crabtree would "take" to me the way she obviously had with Kris. When Dad called out a little later that she'd arrived at our gates I'd worked myself up into quite a lather. I looked out of my window and saw a battered old jeep chugging its way up the drive.

"Wish me luck," I whispered to the photo of Diablo that sits on the windowsill and, taking a deep breath, I ran downstairs to meet her.

CHAPTER EIGHT

T HE JEEP HAD PULLED UP outside and Dad, hand outstretched and smiling, was approaching it. The driver's door opened sharply as if Miss Crabtree had given it a thump (she had – it was the only way it would open, I found out later) and she stepped out. My first reaction was one of anticlimax, she wasn't the six-foot-tall witch-like figure I'd pictured, with gimlet eyes that stared into your deepest soul. Shorter than me, she had pretty silvery hair, tied neatly back and that rosy crumpled skin old people get when they've spent a lot of time outdoors. Her eyes were quite sharp but she looked more my idea of a sweet little old lady than Dean's redoubtable riding guru. I straightened my tie, having dressed in smart jodhpurs, hacking jacket and white shirt, and went forward to meet her, feeling a lot less nervous.

Her handshake was dry and firm and she gave a nod of approval at my appearance. "A little formal for what I have in mind but I'm pleased to see you made the effort Stacey. Now, if you'd like to leave us Mr Jennings, we'll take a look at the horse."

Poor Dad was dying to talk about his plans for the sand school but, despite her innocuous appearance, there was something about Miss

Crabtree that made you do what she said. I showed her into my spotless yard and led Diablo out of his box. I hadn't tacked him up, just brushed the morning's field dust off his gleaming coat. He looked, as always, quite wonderful, and I felt very proud as we paraded round the yard for Miss C's inspection. It seemed to me she was more interested in the way I handled the black horse than in his conformation.

"Dean said you've been having problems," she said. "I thought perhaps there was a clash of temperament but you and Diablo seem on good terms."

"He's an angel," I said, rather soppily. "And I can do anything with him on the ground but as soon as I get in the saddle he changes and doesn't want to do anything I say."

"Let's take him back to his field and I'll show you something."

I was quite taken aback but did as she said because, as I've mentioned, that's the kind of person she is.

Diablo walked beautifully back to the paddock, behaved perfectly with the gate and stood like a rock while I removed his headcollar and gave him a quick cuddle. Then he was off, galloping from a standstill, to join Dolly and Griswald on the far side of the paddock.

"Look." Miss C pointed. "See how supple and

balanced he is. Watch him flick round a right turn, now he's swerving, changing legs three times in three strides and – oh now look what he's doing."

Diablo, as if aware of our watching eyes, was showing off. I suppose it was his way of expressing relief that having been brought in and groomed he was simply being let out to freedom again, not having to go through the battle that our rides together had become. Now he stopped, all four feet together, his head high and tail up like a stallion. He snorted like a dragon and trotted out in an extended gait, sailing across his field like a sleek ocean-going yacht.

"I can't even get an ordinary decent trot out of him," I said enviously. "He just jogs and snatches when I'm on his back. You'd never think he could move like that."

"Dean tells me Diablo's been well trained and so that makes him much easier to confuse than an unschooled horse. If he gets the wrong signals his world almost falls apart and what looks like naughtiness is just frustration."

"Right." I sighed and looked again at the beautiful horse. He'd stopped cavorting and was placidly cropping grass next to Griswald. "Dolly seemed to understand me OK. Does it mean I've blown my chances with Diablo? Won't he ever trust me to ride him properly without upsetting him?"

"Gracious me, of course he will." Miss C patted my arm quite kindly. "It'll take a lot of hard work but I can see you two getting along famously – you've got the basis for it, you obviously love the horse and he's very responsive to you when you're not in the saddle. Dean found him splendid to ride. Once you learn the right aids to give him you'll find you and Diablo will be the perfect partnership."

I felt immensely cheered. The eccentric Miss Crabtree was turning out to be a real pussy cat – a few basic lessons and I'd be back riding the downs without a care in the world.

"So when do we start?" I looked down at my smart attire. "The sand school won't be ready for a week or two but there's a corner of the small paddock we could rope off and – "

"Oh you won't be sitting on Diablo's back for at least a week." Miss Crabtree started walking energetically back to the yard. "I shall come every day and lunge him for a short while, perhaps do some long reining too. Then, when the school is ready, we'll gradually introduce you. Still on the lunge, no stirrups, no reins until I'm satisfied with your seat and your balance. Then we'll start work on those hands."

I gaped at her, not much liking the sound of the regime. "But will that give Diablo enough exercise? Can I still take him out?"

"No, no. He must learn to forget the bad start you two have had. He'll probably need more work to keep him fit so Dean can take him out two or three times a week. I understand part of his work is to help with the stables."

"The stables. Yes." I felt myself getting all pink and furious. "But riding my horse isn't part of the job description. What am I supposed to do while this is going on?"

"You could accompany him on Dolly occasionally," she said calmly. "You're not too big for her and she's getting a little fat. It'll do you both good. Watch Dean and try to carry out the instructions I've given you in your lessons and you'll find even patient, long-suffering Dolly will appreciate it."

To say I was outraged is putting it mildly. This sweet looking little old lady was actually telling me to let someone else ride my wonderful horse while I toddled along behind them on a kiddies' pony. If the someone else hadn't been Dean I'd have told the old dear just what I thought of her game plan. As it was I sort of goggled like a particularly dimwitted goldfish and couldn't find a thing to say. We reached the jeep and there was Dean, looking moody but incredibly handsome. Miss Crabtree smiled. I realised it was for the first time since I'd met her, and I could see how much she liked him.

"All arranged Dean." She spoke briskly but her

sharp old eyes were soft. "Stacey will tell you all about it. She's a very sensible girl, not at all the hothead you described and I think we're going to get along beautifully."

Dean shot me a look of pure surprise and grinned weakly. "Er – good. Miss Crabtree, um, about Kris, you know, the lad last night. I hope he didn't impose – "

"Not at all." She was already climbing into the battered jeep. "He got the job with Mr Lovall by the way. He said to tell you thanks and come round tonight if you like. Oh, and you, Stacey."

I found my voice. "To your house you mean, Miss Crabtree?"

"Yes dear." She spoke as if I was a little lacking mentally. "That's where he lives. About seven then. Goodbye."

And in the loud confusion of a heavily slammed door and protesting gear changes she was gone, bumping up the drive and away. I found myself staring at the space where the jeep had been.

"I knew Lovall would give Kris that job," Dean muttered and kicked the gravel back into place. "Still, at least Miss C's agreed to take you on. I'm glad you liked her."

"I didn't like her at all," I burst out. "When you said eccentric I thought she'd be exciting and different but she's just a cranky old mad woman. I can't believe I agreed to the stuff she said. In fact I don't think I did. She just said it and assumed I'd agreed."

"So if you didn't want to go along with it why didn't you tell her?" Dean asked reasonably.

The main reason was I didn't want to upset him by upsetting her but of course I couldn't tell him that could I, so I said snootily, "I was trying to do what's best for Diablo."

"Good for you." He gave me that sudden, unexpected smile that made my insides turn somersaults. It's not just your heart like they say in the romance novels, but your stomach and all the other floaty bits that leap around when someone who looks like Dean gives you a fabulous, intimate grin.

"So what did you both decide was the best thing for the big black horse?" He was teasing me but it was so great to see his smile I decided the best way of handling this Miss Crabtree thing was to go along with it.

"Well, we've got a good relationship on the ground, so we've just got to forget the bad start with the riding and get the confidence back." I now tried to sound as if the plan was at least partly my idea. "Of course the best way to do that is to start from scratch so I'm just having lessons on the lunge to begin with."

"What about exercising Diablo?" Dean was smart enough to have gone straight to, what was for me, the crux of the matter.

"Oh that can be part of your job," I said as airily as I could. "He goes really well for you doesn't he, you've been taught to ride properly after all, so it makes perfect sense."

"Stacey." He said my name so gently I wanted to cry. "You're really upset by this, aren't you?"

I shook my head fiercely. "No. I was at first but I can see Miss Crabtree's right. I love Diablo and he loves me – but not when I'm riding him. This is the best way. He won't be ruined by my hamfisted technique."

Dean took my hand in his and squeezed it gently. "I think you're brilliant, do you know that?"

The humiliation and anger I'd been feeling were replaced by a heady surge of pure happiness. I didn't want to scare Dean off by being what he'd no doubt think was all soppy over him so I changed the subject before I could get carried away "Thanks pal," I said lightly. "And it's good news about Kris getting the job with Mr Lovall isn't it?"

"I suppose so." He looked moody again. "Though with my luck he won't get put on the Hazelgrove contract so he'll be no use to me. I still can't believe he conned Miss C so easily."

"It didn't sound like a con trick to me," I argued. "He just came straight out and asked if she had a room he could use."

"Yeah, but I didn't hear what else he told her." Dean just wanted to think the worst.

"Well you can find out tonight when we go round to see him."

"You're not coming surely?" He was quite put out. "I need to see him to find out if he'll go along with your suggestion – you know, do a bit of looking round for me when he gets inside the grounds – but you don't have to be there."

"I need to be there to find out just what's going on," I said with great spirit. "Don't tell me you're going to confide in Kris when you won't say a word to me about what's bugging you."

He wouldn't meet my eyes. "Honestly Stacey, it's for the best. You don't want to get mixed up with the kind of stuff I think's going on at Hazelgrove."

"So why do you?" I asked bluntly.

"It's to do with my dad – look I really don't want to talk about it."

"Yet you want to discuss it with Kris and you don't even like him." I felt justified at being mad at him.

"I'm not going to tell him anything, just – um – give him instructions, tell him what to look out for."

"He'll love that won't he," I said sarkily. "Let's face it Dean, you didn't do much to help him,

90

didn't even want him to have the room at Miss C's. All he owes you is the name of a bloke with a job. He's not going to work as an unpaid spy for you just because of that."

"Maybe not," he conceded glumly. "But I don't see what difference you being there with me will make."

"All the difference in the world." I was showing off a bit. "Kris likes me and I reckon he'd do more or less anything I ask him."

"Rubbish. Just because he gave you that corny line about being beautiful. He probably says that to all the girls."

"Hah!" I thought. So he'd noticed Kris's comment! I gave him a brilliant smile, full of secrecy and intrigue.

"Aren't you feeling well?" His immediate, response was sarcastic, but I was sure the attention Kris had paid me was getting to him.

"Don't worry Dean," I leaned forward and ruffled his thick blonde hair. "You're still my favourite."

"Thanks for nothing." He pulled away angrily. "A bit less mickey taking would be appreciated Stacey. I know life's one big game to you but I've got a dad in prison and it's not easy for me to turn everything into a laugh."

I felt immediately contrite, though couldn't help comparing Kris's easy-going way of going about everything despite all the tragedies he'd had to cope with. Dean wasn't the easiest person in the world to get on with, and I could see how his touchiness and quick temper could contribute to his bad reputation. I still liked him an awful lot though and was determined to help him despite the fact he was still shutting me out most of the time. He was uncommunicative for the rest of the day and went home straight after we'd put Diablo in his stable.

"You're sure your dad will drive you over to Miss Crabtree's place?" He was still sulky because I intended going.

"Sure," I said. "And he'll pick me up if I want."

"No, it's OK, I'll walk you back here, it's not far."

He didn't look too thrilled at the prospect so I said wickedly, "Don't bother. I'm sure Kris will be my escort if I ask him."

"I SAID I'd walk with you." His eyes flashed dangerously and I decided to leave off the teasing.

My dad was quite happy to take me to the address Dean had scribbled.

"I've seen that cottage," he said looking at the paper. "Funny little place tucked away at the back of beyond. I'd better pick you up again Stacey. Nine o'clock OK?"

"No, it's all right Dad," I'd spent ages deciding what to wear, but in the end had gone for the look

Dean had admired the day before. "Dean's going to walk me home."

He looked doubtful but didn't argue which showed just how much he trusted Dean. Miss C's cottage was rather tucked away, right at the end of a quiet lane, but it wasn't as far as Dad thought so we arrived ten minutes or so earlier than arranged. Dean wasn't there but Kris, his dark face smiling, was delighted to welcome me in.

"My landlady's gone out," he announced. "Family business she said, which is funny considering she doesn't seem to have any family."

His smile was very infectious. I grinned back and said, "Settled in all right then?"

"Great. She's made me feel really at home. Your parents didn't mind you coming round to see me then? Wild circus boy and all that?"

"No," I said, surprised. "They're pretty lenient and they know where I am. Anyway Dean'll be here soon and my dad thinks he's wonderful."

The black satanic eyebrows raised. "Get away. From what I've been hearing today Dean is the local bad boy."

"Dad says he's been victimised because his father is in prison," I said quickly. "And I think Dean's all right too."

"Yeah I could see that." He grinned knowingly and I felt myself blush.

To hide my embarrassment I did my change-the-subject routine and asked him how he thought he'd like working for Mr Lovall.

He shrugged. "It'll do for now. To be honest what I know about gardening wouldn't cover the back of a seed packet but I don't mind hard work and I'll pick it up as I go along."

"Did you tell Mr Lovall you'd called at Hazelgrove to ask for a job?"

"No, I didn't get past the gate remember, so it wasn't worth mentioning. The funny thing is though that my first job, starting tomorrow, is to help clear some trees in the grounds there."

"Really?" I acted all surprised and felt a surge of elation that the idea I'd had was already showing signs of working. "We'll be next-door neighbours during the day then."

"Lucky me," he touched my hair. "I can't think of anyone I'd like more."

The blush I'd been fighting down deepened and I dropped my eyes quickly. The door bell of Miss Crabtree's cottage pealed suddenly and I turned to answer it, feeling all hot and confused. Dean was outside. He scowled as soon as he saw me, his eyes darting from me to Kris, who was still standing very, very close.

"What are you doing here already?" He almost pushed his way in to stand between Kris and myself.

"My dad dropped me off, like I said he would,"

I snapped, resenting his bossy manner. "And what I'm doing is talking to Kris about his job. Guess where he starts tomorrow?"

"Hazelgrove." Dean said it slowly, still watching me.

I hoped the colour had faded from my face so he wouldn't guess what Kris had been saying. "Yes Hazelgrove. So now maybe you can tell us exactly what you want Kris to do and why."

"No." Dean was always abrupt but this was worse than ever. "I told you I don't want you involved Stacey. I want to talk to Kris alone."

And with that he shoved the startled Kris towards his room at the back of the cottage and shut the door, leaving me firmly outside it!

CHAPTER NINE

D EAN HAD BROUGHT his collie dog, Jack, but I
didn't even have him for company because
he too was inside the room with the lads.

"Typical males!" I thought furiously 'I'll show
them!'

I dare say you've been told, just as I have, that
it's very rude to listen to other people's conversa-
tions and to blatantly eavesdrop is the very height
of bad manners. Tough. I flattened myself against
that door and strained every muscle to find out
what Dean was telling Kris to do. He sounded
rather stiff and pompous which was a sure sign he
wasn't feeling comfortable with the situation.

"I can't give you any reasons I'm afraid," he was
saying. "But I need to find out what's going on at
Hazelgrove and I'd like you to – er – keep your
eyes open while you're working there."

"Would you now?" Kris, in complete contrast,
sounded laid back and slightly amused. "And
what exactly would you like me to be looking
for?"

I held my breath. This was the information I
wanted.

"Um – hard to say," Dean's answer was disappointing. "Anything a bit untoward going on,
particularly around the horses."

"Ah." I could imagine Kris's grin. "Some of Mr Lovall's boys were telling me snooping around the horses is exactly what you were doing when you got thrown out of the place."

"Not really." Dean was defensive. "One of Randall's thugs caught me taking photos. I'm not asking you to do that."

"No you're not. But why exactly are you asking me to do anything at all?" Kris certainly wasn't stupid.

"I can't actually tell you that."

I could hear quite well, though now I realised there was a strange wuffling sound from close by that was blurring the sound of their voices.

It wasn't until Dean said sharply, "What is it Jack? What's bothering you?" that I realised the sound came from the dog, who could obviously sniff my presence, pressed up against the door as I was.

Dean caught on quicker than I did. He wrenched the door open suddenly and I fell forward, staggering almost into his arms.

"Stacey!" He sounded quite shocked. "Were you listening?"

Kris burst into instant laughter. "Of course she was and quite right too! What were you thinking of, locking her out like that?"

I grinned unrepentantly and nonchalantly brushed down my jeans.

Dean gave me his best scowl and said abruptly ,"Stacey's not to be involved."

"Fine by me, mate, because I'm not getting involved either." Kris tweaked my nose in friendly fashion and said "Want a coffee? Or a coke maybe?"

"Thanks." I followed him to the kitchen, ignoring the black looks we were getting from Dean.

Jack pattered out too, plumy tail wagging, so his master didn't have much choice but to join us. We sat round the table with our drinks and Kris talked very entertainingly about his first day at work.

"I was going to pretend I knew how to use a chainsaw," he told us. "But I'm glad I didn't. They're absolutely lethal, I'd have been a danger to every one in a five mile radius."

I laughed. "What are Mr Lovall's merry men using a chain saw for? It hardly comes under the heading of gentle landscaping."

"We're chopping down more trees at the far side of the paddock to the rear."

"Are the horses still in that field? Did you notice how many there were?"

Dean leant forward eagerly, forgetting his sulk.

"Yes they are and no I didn't," Kris glanced at him briefly. "And that's all you're getting."

"Oh Kris." I batted my eyelashes in what I hoped was an appealing fashion. "If Dean tells us what this is all about, you could help him a little couldn't you?"

"But Dean isn't going to let on is he?" The wicked eyes smiled into mine. "And I'm certainly not going to stick my neck out unless there's a really good reason."

"There you are!" I turned to Dean. "Unless you put us both in the picture you're just not going to get anywhere. You can't risk sneaking through our hedging to prowl around Hazelgrove again can you?"

Kris whistled in disbelief. "Phew, you didn't did you? They'll do more than just chuck you out if you try that again."

"I know they will," Dean burst out angrily. "Look what they did to my dad."

There was a brief silence.

"Your dad's in prison for grievous bodily harm or something isn't he?" I asked timidly, knowing how sensitive he was on the subject.

"Dad wasn't doing anything more than a spot of poaching." Dean bent to stroke his dog, so I couldn't see his eyes, but I could see his hands were trembling. "The rest of it, the supposed breaking and entering, was all an invention by Randall and his men."

"It was Hazelgrove he broke into? I didn't know that." I was genuinely surprised.

"You're not listening. No he didn't. He was just

there, in the grounds, nowhere near the house. They stitched him up."

"Why?" Kris asked calmly, as if such a thing were quite a commonplace occurrence.

"He saw something I suppose. I don't know exactly, but I do know he didn't break into the house, he's not a burglar and he didn't beat anyone up. It was the same stunt they pulled on me, only much worse. Randall's men attacked him, not the other way round. They broke two of his ribs and smashed up his face, then said he got the injuries when they had to defend themselves against him."

"But Dean, how do you know?" I asked as gently as I could.

"Dad told me of course. I visited him in prison and he said he wanted me to know he wasn't the villain everyone was making him out to be."

Privately I thought Mr Farraday was bound to say that to his son but I could see Dean really believed him.

"So, your dad knows they set him up to get him put out of the way because of something he saw, right?" Kris was looking a lot more interested now.

"Right." Dean still wouldn't look up.

"So what is it?" Kris asked simply. "Tell me what he saw and OK, I'll tell you if I spot it."

"I don't know." Dean raised his head at last and I could see stark despair in his eyes. "My dad doesn't know himself".

"That doesn't make sense." I couldn't help saying it, and felt so sorry for him as his shoulders sagged in defeat.

"I know but that's the way it is. Dad was in the grounds, he's never denied that, but he was just taking a couple of trout out of the lake. On his way out he heard something and stayed back in the bushes out of sight. They were putting a horse out in the field, he said. He thought it must have been in one of the stables, he hadn't heard a horsebox pull in, so it obviously hadn't just arrived at Hazelgrove."

"What time was this?" I was puzzled. It seemed a strange story to invent, if that's what Mr Farraday had done.

"Early hours of the morning. Dad's always enjoyed the odd spot of poaching and it's something you to tend to do in the dead of night."

"Why on earth would Randall's men be turning horses out at that time?" It didn't make any sense to me. "There wasn't a fire or a flood or something in the stable yard was there?"

"Nothing Dad could see. He wasn't that bothered about why they were doing it, just wanted them to stop doing it and go back to the house."

"So what happened then?" Kris was listening, his dark face hard to fathom.

"Dad hung about for ages till he was sure they'd all gone, then he made his way to the boundary wall. He had to pass quite close to the horses' field and it was there that they jumped him."

"How horrible." I shuddered, thinking of the broken ribs they'd given him in the beating. "And did they call the police straight away and tell them he'd been found breaking in?"

Dean nodded. "They dragged him into the house and locked him in a downstairs room. Then they obviously went off and reported to Randall. Next thing Dad knows is the window being smashed from the outside and the sound of someone being thumped."

"What? D'you mean somebody tried to help him escape?" I stared at him in amazement.

"I think this was the break-in being set up." Kris was brighter than me about these things. "They were going to call the police so they had to make it look as though Mr Farraday had got in by smashing the window."

I frowned. "So who was getting beaten up?"

Dean shrugged. "One of Randall's gorillas. Their story was that Dad broke in with burglary in mind and he attacked this bloke when he tried to stop him. Of course all my dad could do was deny it, because there wasn't a word of truth in it, but with the evidence they'd faked building up against him, everyone thought he was just lying."

"And that meant once he was established as an out and out villain and liar no one would believe him if he told what he'd seen out in the grounds." Kris looked almost appreciative. "That's pretty clever."

"Clever my eye," I said crossly, annoyed I wasn't very good at working out mysteries. "Dean says his dad didn't see anything so why should Randall go to all this trouble?"

"It must be something to do with this horse, the one being moved out of the yard at that time of night. Randall wouldn't want to take the risk of Mr Farraday having seen whatever it is, so the best way of making his testimony worthless was to get the law on his side. The police weren't likely to take Mr Farraday's word against Randall and his staff."

"I think that's dead right." Dean looked at Kris with grudging admiration. "Dad was already known as a bit of a lad, nothing serious, and he'd never ever use violence, I absolutely know that, but with all that evidence against him, he didn't stand a chance. Even the rest of my family think he's guilty."

"But not you, Dean," I said softly and he gave me the ghost of that wonderful smile.

"No, not me. I believe he's innocent and I'm going to prove it."

"So that's why you were taking photographs of

the horses? Not to copy them in your painting?"

He shot me a scornful look. "I never use photos, always paint from the real thing or sketches I've made. I've got a good memory for colour and form."

"What was so interesting about the group of horses in the paddock that day?" I wondered.

He shrugged. "Nothing that I could see, though I didn't get very close."

"I think whatever they're trying to hide is more likely to be in the stableyard," Kris said. "Though one thing's for sure, the Randall setup don't want any form of snooping round whatsoever. Stacey says they were pretty rough on you."

"I got off lightly compared to my dad." Dean scratched Jack's head absent mindedly and the collie thumped his tail on the floor. "But again, they weren't going to risk having me around were they? Poor old Lovall, he didn't know my dad was in prison for breaking into Hazelgrove. I bet they gave him hell when they realised I was on his payroll. They've probably had you checked out, Kris."

"Nothing to find there," Kris said cheerfully. "No family, no record, no nothing. I didn't even tell Mr Lovall about the circus, just made up a background he'll be comfortable with."

"You see, that's another strange thing." I frowned, trying to get into detective mode. "Why should Mr Randall's name be mentioned in a circus. I can't see what connection he could possibly have."

"Maybe he bought horses from Tony Cinquetti from time to time," Kris suggested. "Tony did a lot of that sort of thing."

"I don't think circus horses would be in Randall's line at all," I said thoughtfully. "I've never met him but I know he specialises in very high-bred animals. He wants to become a top three-day eventer so they'd have to be show jumpers and do dressage and cross-country."

"There's nothing to get hold of is there?" Kris agreed, passing round biscuits. "Any lead we come up with takes us nowhere and we don't have a single clue to speak of."

"So you still won't help?" Dean's face looked stiff where he was trying to hide his disappointment. "I suppose you think it's not worth it, just a stupid story made up by a lying crook. People who know my dad don't believe him so why should you?"

"I believe you though," Kris said surprisingly. "And if you say he isn't lying then that's good enough for me. I was close to my father too, you know."

For a moment the jokey, wicked mask slipped and I could see only sadness in his dark eyes. I opened my mouth to sympathise but he'd already snapped back to his usual cheeky self.

"So, Stacey. You're the educated one. I'll get some paper and you can draw up a plan of campaign."

I gawped at him. "Plan of – I wouldn't have a clue."

"And as I said, a clue is definitely what we need." Kris grabbed a notebook and pen. "Right. Point one: obviously I'll have to keep my eyes peeled. I don't think Mr Lovall is ever told to do any work in the stableyard area but if there's any chance of getting in there for a look I'll take it."

"Be careful Kris." Dean was already looking more cheerful. "Any excuse and they'll chuck you out. You could try asking the other blokes who work for Lovall if they've seen anything. They've been doing the landscaping at Hazelgrove ever since Randall bought it and they might have noticed something. I didn't get to talk to them that much."

"No problem. They're already yacking away like old mates with me." Kris grinned and I realised that that was his usual effect on people. He was so friendly, such good company, you felt immediately relaxed with him as if you'd known him all your life.

I smiled at both of them and said proudly, "I've thought of something. You know we're having this sandschool put in – well Mr Randall's got a beautiful all-weather school, I know because Mrs Locke, our cleaner, is sister-in-law to Mr Randall's cleaner and she told her and she told me."

"Very succinctly put." Kris laughed and ruffled my hair again.

Dean scowled, whether it was an automatic reflex or whether it bothered him every time Kris did that, I don't know. "So, where does all that lead us?"

"I could get Dad to ask Mr Randall if we could have a look at his manege," I explained. "You know, a neighbourly thing, we're having one built, can we see how yours looks, kind of stuff. Randall won't have any reason to suspect us will he? And I might even get to see round the yard."

"I could go and see my dad again," Dean said slowly. "It's a long journey and I haven't been for a while. He might have remembered something that would help."

We talked and talked but didn't come up with much more. In the end Dean said he ought to be walking me back so that my dad wouldn't start worrying. He's such a gentleman isn't he. We said goodbye to Kris and left him washing up our cups. The two lads are so well behaved sometimes it makes me laugh. As we reached the end of the lane we heard the rattle and clatter of Miss Crabtree's old jeep and she waved in a friendly way as she passed us. I thought about her plan to let Dean ride Diablo and pushed it away quickly. Dean, who seemed much happier now he'd shared his secret at last, was quite chatty on the way home. He's a much quieter personality than Kris and hadn't had so much to say back at the cottage, but I think he was more comfortable when it was just me and him. Jack trotted along at his side, intelligent head cocked and ears constantly moving as he listened to the countryside sounds.

They left me at my gates and I skipped up the drive, feeling strangely elated. I did realise Dean's problem wasn't an easy one to resolve, and in fact had my doubts that three teenagers would be able to do enough to sort it out. Still, the closeness that was developing between Dean and me was enough to put a glow over almost anything, and I must admit I was also enjoying the attention I got from Kris.

"I hope we solve the Hazelgrove mystery" I told myself as I drifted off to sleep. "But, without wanting to be mean to Mr Farraday, I hope we don't solve it too soon!"

CHAPTER TEN

DURING THE NEXT FEW DAYS it looked as though the second part of that wish was proving a reality. Kris asked as many questions and did as much prowling about as he dared, but came up with nothing. He was still pinning his hopes on a snoop round the stable yard, but his work never took him there, and someone was always around.

"It's as though Randall's men are on the lookout all the time," he said. "They always know exactly where we're meant to be and they make sure we stay put. They told Mr Lovall none of us were to touch any of the horses or even go near the paddocks and stables."

"What exactly are these guys?" I asked irritably. "I know Hazelgrove's a big place, they've got more acreage than we have, but what do these men of Randall's do all day? He's got Mr Lovall's firm for his grounds and he hasn't got enough horses for them all to be grooms."

"I think they're bodyguards," Kris said. "No, don't laugh, I do really. Whenever we see Randall around and whenever he goes out he has at least one of those guys with him and the others stay and watch the house like a couple of Rottweilers."

Dean and I laughed, it was a good description. I was pinning my hopes on the visit my dad said he'd arrange with Mr Randall. It had taken a bit of persuading to get him to phone.

"I don't particularly want to look at Hazelgrove's manege," he'd said. "One of the chaps Dean sent along has the plans for an ideal sand school for us."

"But Mr Randall has dressage exhibitions and – er – stuff in his," I argued. "I'd love to see what it's like."

Poor Dad looked puzzled at this sudden interest in the formerly despised word "dressage" but as usual agreed to go along with what I wanted. Mr Randall wasn't in when he called and it was a couple of days before he phoned back. It proved to be a disappointing call.

"He says he'd love us to call round sometime," Dad reported. "But not at the moment. Apparently he's having some work done on the school and it's a bit of a mess."

Kris hadn't said anything about that and I checked with him later.

"Not true." His dark eyes sparkled with interest. "Well, we haven't learnt much have we, but one thing's for sure. Whatever Mr Randall has got at Hazelgrove he's determined to keep anyone from seeing it. We're just going to have to come up with a better plan."

It was easier said than done though and the days went by without any breakthrough. Life at

Deepdene was going on apace in the meantime. Miss Crabtree turned up every day, at first taking Diablo off on her own to lunge him, then when she was satisfied with his performance, she put me on his back. I had no reins and no stirrups and I felt very odd and very, very precarious. My leg position was completely wrong, she said, even without irons I tended to swing my lower leg forward and grip like a monkey with my knees. I was even sitting incorrectly and had to work really hard to change the habits of a lifetime (OK, six years then). My hips had to be square with Diablo's and Miss C said I should be able to feel the weight of my body being carried equally on both seat bones. Apparently I was both backward tilting and lopsided! So, struggling to keep backside and legs in what was, to me, a totally alien position, I then had to learn that my upper body, while in a nice straight line (ear, shoulder, hip and back of heel) must be supple and without tension. I'm not kidding – I had enough tension to rival a stretched elastic band, but I gritted my teeth (actually I didn't – that creates even more tension) and tried and TRIED.

Oddly enough I didn't mind Dean taking Diablo out nearly as much as I thought I would. The first time I felt funny, jealous and a bit tearful, but by the time they came walking beautifully back into the yard, I'd given myself a good talking-to and was able to greet them with a cheerful smile. Diablo had obviously enjoyed himself so I resigned myself to just accompanying the horse of my dreams on his hacks out, just till Miss Crabtree considered I was good enough to ride him myself. Dolly was a little surprised at her return to work but she treated it with her usual stoic patience. Griswald always got a nice little bucket of titbits to console him when we went out so quite frankly he couldn't care less about being left.

On the rides out I tried to put into practise everything I was learning in our lovely new sand school. We took it very gently at first. Dolly wasn't yet back to full fitness and Diablo still had a tendency to try and bomb off if we went faster than a collected canter. It was still good fun though, out in the crisp early winter air, feeling the wind in your face and breathing in its salt-laden tang of the sea. Dean said one day soon we'd take the horses down to the beach which was only a few miles away, so Diablo could have a gallop along the sand.

"Dolly would like that too." I patted her neck fondly. "I don't think she's ever been to the seaside."

"Unlike poor old Griswald," Dean laughed. "Now he definitely wouldn't appreciate a trip to the beach."

"He'd pass out at the thought of being made to

work again," I agreed and laughed with him.

It was good to see him relaxed and happy for once. He didn't say much about how he was feeling, but I knew the pain was still deep. The visit to his dad wasn't for another week and he was hoping against hope that it would produce the vital, much needed clue. Kris hadn't given up but he'd drawn a blank from Mr Lovall's men. They hadn't seen anything untoward, though they agreed Randall was an "odd un". Their opinion was that anyone with money tends to be a bit strange. As a somewhat rich person myself I disputed this with Kris.

"Calm down, my fiery little gypsy," he teased, as always. "They just mean the wealthy tend to use their money for what seems to the likes of us labourers to be pretty daft things."

"Such as?" I challenged.

"Well, in Randall's case it seems to be all things horsey. He's spent a fortune putting in that indoor manege. It is smart, I grant you, I've had a sneaky look round and it's beautifully done. Seating for spectators, teaching area for lectures, hospitality room, the lot. And what's he doing now? Only getting us to fell a load of trees, clear another complete area right at the back of the grounds to put in another school."

"Another school?" I repeated, bemused. "What ever for?"

"Exactly. It's not on the same scale, this is an outdoor one, more like the one you've got, but it does seem a bit excessive."

"I should say." I shook my head. "It's like everything else, it doesn't make sense. Nothing about this Hazelgrove mystery makes sense."

"And that's exactly what makes it such an intriguing little affair." Kris's eyes were sparkling again. He obviously enjoyed a challenge.

"I think it all centres on Randall himself." I tried to apply some lateral thinking. "He's a real mystery man isn't he. According to Mrs Locke he started off by acting the lord of the manor, big parties, all the local top nobs invited. She says he fancies himself as a country gentleman, wants to be part of the horsey county set. That's why he built the manege, but Mrs Locke's sister-in-law says none of the real topnotch people want to know. They find all that beastly money spending rather vulgar she thinks."

Kris laughed. "I wish I could be that vulgar. Actually though, Miss Crabtree says almost the same thing. She was outraged when Randall 'sent for her' as she puts it, and more or less demanded she found him a sure fire push-button type of horse he'd be guaranteed to win three-day events with."

"I didn't know that." I was highly entertained at the thought of anyone trying to make the awesome Miss C do anything. I'd stopped saying anything other than "yes Miss Crabtree" weeks ago. "What did she say?"

"What do you think? She told him in no uncertain terms the first thing he must do is learn to ride properly. Apparently he has hands like sides of beef and sits in the saddle as though he's got cement in his underwear."

I giggled delightedly. "She didn't tell him that did she?"

"Oh yes and more besides. I'd like to have been a fly on the wall that day."

"Me too. When was all this? Not recently?"

"No, it was when Randall first arrived, before you got here. Miss Crabtree used to receive an invitation to his horsey evenings but not after that obviously."

"That's a shame in a way. If anyone is going to spot something adrift with those horses, it'd be her. She doesn't miss a thing."

"You know the more I think about this, the more I'm convinced it doesn't have anything to do with the horses themselves." Kris had gone all thoughtful. "It would make far more sense for there to have been some sort of criminal activity going on the night Dean's dad went a-poaching."

"Criminal?" I was incredulous. "But you've just said Randall's rolling in money. Why would there be anything like that going on?"

"We don't know how he makes his money do we?" Kris pointed out.

"Oh you think he might be some sort of gangster, do you?" I was taking the mickey.

"Could be. His thugs, as Dean likes to call them, would definitely look more at home in some sleazy nightclub than plodding through the countryside mud down here. Whatever they are, they're definitely not horsey sorts which is another reason we should be looking elsewhere for our clues."

"I'll find out exactly how Randall makes his money shall I?" I looked at his doubtful face and laughed. "Honestly Kris you're getting as bad as Dean. He's always trying to stop me 'getting involved' in case I get myself into bother. You're overprotective, the pair of you."

"Not me." Kris showed his white teeth in a wolf's grin. "I just don't want lover boy having a go at me for not stopping you. How exactly do you intend finding out about Randall?"

"I shall do what all good little girls do and ask my dad," I said demurely. "He seems a vague old thing I know, but he's really very astute. I bet he knows a lot about our dear neighbour already."

He did, as it happened, and the next day I was able to give a full report to the two lads when we met up at Miss Crabtree's cottage.

"Guess where I've been today," I greeted them

cockily. "Only Mr Randall's art gallery that's all!"

"Art – you mean you've been inside Hazelgrove?" Dean's frown nearly made his eyebrows disappear. "Oh Stacey, you must be careful – "

"No, not in his house." I shut him up before he could get started on me. "I asked Dad what kind of business Randall was in and he said straight-away that he owned an art gallery. You know, one of those posh shops just selling pictures."

"Yes Stacey," Dean's voice was resigned. "Even peasants like Kris and I have heard of them."

"Pooh to you," I said charmingly and went on, "Dad said he'd actually seen the gallery – it's in Barringford – so of course I wanted to see it too."

"And of course Daddy said yes," Dean and Kris spoke together.

I put my tongue out at the pair of them and said, "If you don't want to know about my detective work just keep right on sending me up."

"No, we want to hear." Dean patted the ever accompanying Jack. "Go on."

"It's quite a big place, but tucked away a bit, off the main shopping area. Some quite nice pictures, prints mostly and everything framed in those heavy ornate mouldings."

"Lovely," Dean said, whether being sarcastic or not I couldn't tell. "So what did you find out?"

"Well it's obvious isn't it. The art business is

117

renowned for fakes. Mr Randall deals in forgeries, that's how he makes all that money."

There was a pause.

"Is that it?" Kris looked disgusted. "I thought you'd come up with something more concrete than that."

"I think it's good," I argued. "Why else would someone like Randall have a gallery tucked away in a quiet little town like Barringford? He's the flash type isn't he, something opulent in central London's more his scene surely."

"The gallery's probably something on the lines of a hobby," Dean said wearily. "People like him have no real taste and that type of place can cater for his banal choice of so-called art. It can't have anything to do with what my dad saw that night."

"Yes it can." I'd worked it all out. "The night your dad went poaching I reckon a buyer turned up at Hazelgrove to see one of the forged or stolen paintings. Because Randall wouldn't risk keeping hot items in the house itself the pictures are stored in the stables. Your dad witnessed them turning a horse out of the yard and into the field in the dead of night. Why would they do that unless they needed to get at something which had been stored somewhere in that horse's loosebox?"

They both stared at me, stunned. I sat back smugly. That was more like it.

"She can't possibly be right." Dean looked at

Kris, who lifted his shoulders and shook his head theatrically.

"It's so outrageous, it could be," he said. "If there was a tip-off the last place anyone would look would be under the floor of a stable that had a horse living in it."

"Let me get this straight." Dean looked at me. "You're saying Randall owns this art gallery place as a front, and when he gets a buyer who wants something special he has a secret supply of stolen paintings that he keeps in the stableyard at Hazelgrove? No way, it's pure fiction. Why doesn't he store them – I don't know – in the cellar underneath the gallery or something?"

"Because that's the first place anyone would look," Kris said slowly "Whereas the stable – "

"Is the last place. Yeah, yeah I know, you said." Dean was getting irritable. "So what am I supposed to ask my dad next week? Whether he happened to see one of the thugs strolling round the grounds with a nice copy of the Mona Lisa tucked under his arm? I think he might have remembered that don't you?"

"That's the whole point," I said impatiently. "Your dad really didn't see anything he hasn't told you. What Randall didn't want anyone believing was that the horse was turned out at night. He wanted the police to think Mr Farraday went straight to the house and broke the window NOT that he was out in the grounds. Randall didn't want attention focused on the stableyard, that's why they pretended it was the house that was broken into."

"I always thought the whole thing centred on the yard." Kris slapped his hand down on the table. "No wonder they make sure Lovall's men, or anyone else come to that, don't go anywhere near it."

"And no wonder the invitations to the dressage evenings have dried up," I reminded them. "And that Randall wouldn't agree to Dad and I going over there to take a look at the manege. It all fits, Dean."

CHAPTER ELEVEN

DEAN STILL DIDN'T look convinced. It was Saturday morning and all three of us (plus Jack of course) were in the hay loft at Deepdene. It's a nice warm place to meet up in the winter and as Kris didn't work at weekends, the ideal spot to discuss developments. Dean was setting up an easel by the window. He said the light was almost as good as being outside. I watched with interest. I'd had a sneaky look at several of his sketches, which I thought were terrific, but this was the first painting I'd been near.

It was a watercolour of the first thing I'd seen him draw – the group of horses in the paddock at Hazelgrove. The background was all hazy greens and golds and the soft blue-grey of an autumn sky, but the horses were more sharply defined. A couple of handsome bays, an undistinguished looking grey and a skewbald, whose fine lines I'd already commented on. Dean's touch with a paintbrush was a joy to watch, delicate but very sure, the colours springing to life under his hand.

Kris was lolling back in the straw, legs stretched before him, hands behind his head. He was looking out of the window while he gave us a vivid, blow by blow account of how he'd spent most of the previous day wrestling a huge tree root out of the area being cleared for Hazelgrove's new sandschool. A mundane subject you'd have thought, but with Kris telling the story it was absolutely hilarious. He got to his feet at one point so he could demonstrate a particularly funny position he'd got himself into, and immediately broke off the narrative to wave and shout in friendly fashion at someone below.

"Miss C's outside." He turned back from the window. "She's finished lunging Diablo and she's coming up."

"What?" Dean stopped painting immediately. "You can't just yell out and ask Miss Crabtree up here!"

"Why not? I just did," Kris pointed out equably.

"But – but – " I stammered, obviously feeling exactly the same as Dean. "What are we going to do with her?"

Jack, who'd become an ace at swarming up the loft ladder, stood at the trap door and barked. I'm sure he was saying he wasn't too keen either. A minute or two later Miss Crabtree's sweet, silvery head appeared.

She shot me one of her looks and said, "Dolly looks as though she's sweated up this morning, Stacey. You and Dean haven't been tearing around the downs have you?"

"No Miss Crabtree." Dean respectfully offered her his arm to climb up the last step. She waved it away and energetically clambered into the loft.

"We just cantered." I always sounded so defensive when I spoke to the old lady but that was because I was. "Dolly's still just a bit chubby so she gets very hot, but we walked all the way back to cool them down didn't we Dean?"

"Oh yes." He was like me, almost standing to attention.

Kris, in complete contrast as usual, had gone back to lolling. He even patted the straw next to him and invited Miss C to sit down. She refused but to my surprise there was a fond twinkle in her eye that definitely wasn't there when she looked at me (or even Dean). She chatted away quite amiably though, and even went so far as to say I was doing better than she expected with the riding lessons. Praise indeed! I felt quite light headed and, to hide my pleasure and embarrassment, walked over to Dean's painting and asked her what she thought of it. As soon as I saw Dean's scowl I knew it was the wrong thing to have done. Being Miss Crabtree, there was no instant "Ooh isn't it lovely", but several minutes silence, while she stood and gravely inspected the half-finished watercolour. Eventually she pronounced it very good, and I saw Dean's shoulders sag with relief. "But of course the skewbald's all wrong," she said in her usual brisk tones. "But I suppose that's because you're doing it from memory."

Dean flushed brick red and mumbled about having an excellent memory.

I rushed in clumsily, desperate to save him from further criticism. "It must be right, Dean got a good look at the horses, even took photos only of course they got ruined. You know the skewbald do you, Miss Crabtree?"

"No," she looked mildly surprised. "Does he belong to someone local?"

"He's one of Mr Randall's," I knew I ought to shut up but I couldn't. "You've been to Hazelgrove haven't you?"

"A while ago I did, but there was no skewbald." Miss C cast a shrewd eye on the still glowering Dean. "Randall was a dreadful man I thought, but you're on the right track if you want to impress him for some reason. He knows nothing about real horses in my opinion, but he has the biggest collection of painted ones I've ever seen. Are you doing this picture for him, Dean?"

"No I'm not." Dean was clenching and unclenching his fingers, oblivious of the paintbrush he still held.

"No, I thought that couldn't be it, with the trouble your poor father got into at Hazelgrove. I know you're taking his imprisonment very hard, Dean, but I think you'd be well advised to leave Randall alone."

Kris, whose usually wicked face had suddenly

become the picture of innocence, put in quickly, "Oh Dean's painting's just a hobby, isn't it mate? It's just a coincidence this being a picture of Randall's horses. Don't you worry Miss C, we're not up to anything and we're certainly not going near Mr Randall. Now d'you want to go along to the house and Stacey will make you a nice cup of coffee?"

I glared at him in horror, but to my relief Miss Crabtree refused.

"No thank you Kris." She tried to sound severe but you could see she didn't mean it. "And I hope you're telling the truth for once. You three seem to be in a permanent huddle and I'd hate to think you're plotting anything that could get Dean in trouble."

"Thanks Miss Crabtree." Dean stopped fuming when she said that and looked at her quite fondly. "You've always backed me up and I appreciate it."

"Just be sensible and don't go along with too many of this young man's schemes." She actually patted Kris's head. "The trouble is he's a bit too bright for his own good."

"And you love me for it." Kris was irrepressible, and I think he'd have given the fierce old lady a hug if he'd been standing up.

She may have thought so too because she backed away looking a bit flustered and said she had to be going. Kris helped her down the ladder,

125

even though she said she didn't need him to, and came back up, whistling cheerfully.

"Hark at him," Dean said bitterly. "Not a care in the world. Nice one, Kris, inviting Miss Crabtree up here. She's not daft, she's already worked out we're up to something."

"She's a lovely old duck." (Definitely Kris's description not mine!) "You're just annoyed she didn't like your pretty picture. Let me have a look at it." He stood with his head to one side and regarded the painting solemnly. "Funny thing really, some of the guys in the circus called coloured horses like this, paints or painted horses. So this could be a painting of a painted horse if you like. Anyway, Miss C is wrong and you're right. I see this horse every day, only from across the field I grant you, but it's a good likeness. The grey's spot on as well."

"Thank you," Dean looked mollified. "And the two bays? Are they still there?"

"Yeah, it's good of them too, oh and there's a lighter one as well, but come to think of it he only arrived last week so you wouldn't have seen him. He's going to be Randall's event horse apparently."

"Really?" I was immediately interested. "How do you know that?"

"I heard him tell my boss. Don't know why he did really. Old Lovall isn't the least bit interested

126

in horses and Randall hardly ever bothers to pass the time of day with him usually. But heh, my fellow sleuths, did you happen to take note of what dear Miss C said?"

"About what?" Dean was still scowling at his watercolour.

"About the painted horses. She said Randall's got a fine collection of horse pictures. That might tie in with Stacey's idea about forgeries and the art gallery and so on."

"You think so?" Dean was chewing his thumb nail. "Look, we've just got to get a proper look at that yard. The horses are turned out all day aren't they, so it shouldn't be that hard to search the stables once we get inside the yard."

"And how do you propose getting inside the yard?" Kris demanded. "The whole place is guarded like a fortress, any visitors are escorted round the grounds by Randall and his shadow, so if even invited guests aren't allowed to wander round, what chance do we have?"

"Maybe I could get in by disguising myself." Dean was getting desperate.

"What as? The milkman? You wouldn't get further than the kitchen door."

"How about if you sling a brick through one of the stable windows and I turn up to repair it?"

"Don't be so stupid." I stopped him, feeling quite alarmed. "A harebrained scheme like that isn't going to work and there's no way you could disguise yourself successfully as anything, Dean. They know exactly what you look like, and Kris too of course. But – " I paused, thinking hard.

"But what?" They said in unison.

"They don't know me. I could pretend to be a student of architecture or something and ask to look at the yard because it was – I don't know – built in a particularly unusual style or it's a good example of Victorian craftsmanship."

"Sure, sure," Kris nodded sarkily. "Except Randall had it built when he moved in – it's as interesting architecturally as a modern housing estate."

"Anyway it's completely out of the question, Stacey. You are not to set foot on Hazelgrove's land, not under any pretext whatsoever." Dean was frowning and looking all macho. "It's far too dangerous for a girl."

"Especially this particular girl apparently." Kris smiled sweetly and I stamped my foot at both of them.

"Oh for goodness sake stop treating me as if I'm all soft and fluffy. I'm neither and if I got into Hazelgrove I could look after myself."

"No, Stacey." Dean looked really worried "That's just it, you couldn't. These are not nice people we're dealing with."

As if I hadn't worked that out for myself! I

glowered at him but stayed quiet and just went on plotting and scheming. I could see Kris grinning, he knew exactly what was going on in my mind and I felt irrationally annoyed with him too. He didn't order me around the way Dean did but he had no more faith in my ability to sort out this mystery. What it came down to was that they both thought I was a spoilt little daddy's girl who'd never had to fight her own battles. I suppose that was true as far as it went, but I was made of stronger stuff than they imagined and I was determined to get things moving. I stomped home, still feeling irritable, and met Dad who was pottering around happily in the garden. He loved Deepdene and had always thoroughly enjoyed doing all the jobs he was now paying Dean to do. I felt a pang of remorse. If I hadn't insisted on going to Dean's aid the day he got thrown out of Hazelgrove, Dad would still have his beloved grounds all to himself.

"Hiyah Dad." I tried to shake off my bad mood and let him know he was appreciated. "It all looks very smart everywhere."

"That's young Dean's ministrations, not mine," he said ruefully. "It would have taken me half the winter to get all these jobs done."

"And you'd have loved it," I thought sympathetically. Aloud I said, "Oh well, Dean's becoming more involved with the horses now. I expect there will be plenty of work for you in the Spring won't there?"

"Oh yes," he brightened at the thought. "Your mother wants a herb garden put in and I think I'd like a lake or at least a pond. Plenty to do. With luck we'll be able to keep Dean and myself busy."

"Dad, you're very good to have taken him on," I burst out impulsively. "I know you're just being kind – I'm not sure why but Dean certainly appreciates it and so do I."

"Thank you my pet." He looked quite touched, I'm not usually good at saying stuff like that. "You seem to be maturing rather nicely if I may say so. I'll tell you why I'm so keen to give Dean some support. I checked him out, as I told you, and he really isn't a bad lad you know. Nearly all his troubles stem from who he is – the son of Jake Farraday."

"So his dad's a real villain then?"

"So it seems. He's always had a reputation, and a police record come to that, but nothing serious till this last nasty case at Hazelgrove. The point is, whatever he's like – it's not Dean's fault. That boy is suffering because of something that's not of his own making. A bad father does not necessarily mean a bad son. I should know."

I looked at him in surprise. "You – ?"

"Your grandad Jennings was always in trouble," he said quietly. "I had to move away from my home town in the end. No one would ever give me a chance, or have a good word for me."

I goggled. I'd had no idea. "Poor Dad. Is that why we've moved around so much – to get away?"

"Oh no. Once I got a good job I worked twice as hard as anyone else just to prove I was nothing like my father. Don't get me wrong, I loved my dad, as much as Dean loves his, but there came a time when I had to face facts. We moved a few times because I was so ambitious, just had to keep building the businesses up to prove it wasn't a fluke. But I'm content now, I love it here, don't need to keep working, and I'm happy to stay put. When I heard about Dean it brought it all back, that's why I felt I had to give him a helping hand, if only in a small way."

"You're terrific, d'you know that." I hugged him warmly. "And, like I say, we appreciate it."

It was on the tip of my tongue to tell him about Randall's setup which had put Mr Farraday behind bars, but in the end I decided not to. He'd have been sceptical about Dean's unshakeable belief in his dad's innocence and, let's face it, we had no evidence whatsoever. Of course Dad knew Dean had been thrown out of Hazelgrove on a trumped up excuse but he thought that was because they didn't want a jailbird's son working for them. It was a pity, because my dad is a person who gets things done, but I knew now wasn't the moment to ask for his help. I was just going to have to get some proof myself. (And show Dean and Kris what a fantastic person I was as a bonus).

I left Dad in the garden and stopped off to say hello to my beloved horses. Diablo and Dolly had been particularly wonderful on the morning's ride. The grey pony seemed to appreciate the new, improved rider I was becoming, and was thoroughly enjoying her trips out. I'd decided even when I was back riding Diablo I'd still use Dolly too. I could get someone to share her, and of course there was no reason Dean couldn't still ride Diablo sometimes. I had this lovely, romantic vision of us galloping together on the shore, laughing as the wind whipped the waves into foam at our feet and seagulls shrieked and swooped overhead. Our horses would be moving fluidly in a perfect gait, Diablo's gleaming black muscles rippling, a perfect foil for the pretty, rounded outline that was the smaller grey mare. A study in black and white, Dean's blonde, wind tossed hair contrasting dramatically with the dark smoky mass of my own, as the horses seemed to fly through the glittering spray.... Yeah, yeah, I know, in reality Diablo would be about a mile ahead of Dolly, we'd have hats on so our hair wouldn't be blowing in the wind and anyway it would probably be raining! You have to admit my dream picture's much nicer.

I'd always loved riding, even the scare of being run away with by Diablo hadn't put me off, and now I was learning so much more about it, my enjoyment was increasing. I even harboured secret ambitions of competing, cross-country perhaps, show jumping and even dressage. There was a big event coming up in the New Year and I was determined to go along as a spectator and get some idea of what it was all about. I told Diablo this, whispering in his silky ear as he gently took the pieces of apple I'd bitten off for him.

"We'll be there one day Diablo." I buried my face into his neck, breathing in the sweet smell of him.

He whickered and nudged me as if in agreement.

"I see you two are getting on better than ever." I thought Miss Crabtree had left, but apparently she'd been in the house drinking coffee with my mum. "It won't be long before you're similarly attuned when you're riding," she went on. "As I told you, you're really coming on quite well, Stacey."

"Thanks Miss Crabtree." She never, ever praised unless you deserved it, so I felt quite humble. "It's nice to know my days of being run away with by my black devil horse are over." I said it quite lightly, to hide the pleasure I was feeling, and was surprised when with a sudden "ping" an idea hit me. I was so excited I almost blurted it out in front of Miss Crabtree and that would never have done. Instead I made a strange gargling noise and she looked at me with concern.

"What did you say, Stacey?"

Hurriedly I launched into speech "Er – I was thinking of going along to the three-day event at Branwell that's on soon. What do you think? It's –um – good quality isn't it?"

"Very good." She glanced at me shrewdly. I'm sure she guessed that wasn't what I'd been about to say. "Though in my opinion the standard's been lowered by the inclusion of an entry from your neighbour."

"Oh?" As usual I was very interested. "Mr Randall's taking part is he? I suppose this will be his first competition with this new horse he's bought."

"A very indifferent animal," Miss C sniffed. "Though still far too good for Randall. They certainly won't be winning. You'll do better to watch virtually anyone else."

I made noises of agreement and watched with relief as she finally set off for her jeep. I just couldn't wait to think the brilliant idea through and I certainly didn't want Miss Crabtree around for that!

CHAPTER TWELVE

I GAVE THE HORSES one last cuddle and charged back to the house to work out my plan. It was the throwaway remark I'd made to Miss C that inspired it and you'll see why she was the last person I could discuss it with. In fact, the more thought I gave it, the more I realised I couldn't really tell anyone. Dean was definitely out of the question with his attitude about me getting involved, and as for talking to Kris – ? I wasn't sure about him. At first I thought he might play a part in my scheme, but thinking about the way he joined in the "spoilt little girly" routine, I decided against it. Anyway it would be brilliant to see the look on his and Dean's face when I nonchalantly told them I'd not only got into Hazelgrove's stableyard, but I'd solved the whole mystery! Nothing if not confident, that's me.

So, having decided to go through with the idea completely alone, the next thing was to decide which day would be best. Obviously not one when Dean was around, and it would be better if Dad wasn't on the scene either. He's another one who's overprotective. Honestly men are a real pain sometimes. I remembered Dad had offered to drive Dean to the Barringford coach station on Tuesday and thought excitedly that it would make a perfect opportunity. Dean was off for the day on his prison visit to his father, and my dad had announced he'd probably spend the day in Barringford,where there were one or two people he wanted to see. So, Tuesday morning it would be then. I closed my eyes to concentrate. There'd be no riding out with Dean away, but Miss C would be arriving at nine for my lesson on Diablo. She rarely hung about afterwards, so she'd be gone by ten. I could fiddle about in the stable pretending to untack the black horse and then when she was gone – I shivered in anticipation. To make what I was planning to do believable from the Hazelgrove point of view, a lot depended on local gossip. Dean knew only too well the way local people loved to discuss their neighbours. He'd said ruefully that at the height of the tittle-tattle about his family, he only had to sneeze in the morning and by noon half a dozen people had asked him how his cold was!

My scheme was going to be helped, I thought, by the single fact that Mrs Locke's sister-in-law did the cleaning for Mr Randall. Neither woman was even slightly interested in horses, but oh how they loved a good gossip about people. Mrs Locke was forever commenting on my riding ability, or lack of it, even though she wouldn't know a half pass from a pirouette. Now I was having lessons from the local high priestess of equitation, Mrs

Locke would be delightedly informing anyone who'd listen (and I was hoping her sister-in-law was among these) that at long last something was being done about the terrible way I went tearing around on that maniacal black horse of mine. As long as Mr Randall's cleaner had imparted this information to her employer, and if she was anything like Mrs Locke she'd tell him whether he wanted to know or not, my strategy for getting into Hazelgrove's yard would seem perfectly genuine. All I had to do was pretend to be schooling Diablo after Miss Crabtree had left, and get run away with again! Only this time the black horse would gallop across Deepdene's field till he came to the hedge, which he'd go soaring over to land in Hazelgrove's grounds!

I'd be in perfect control of course, though doing theatrical girly screams to make the right effect. Then I'd let Diablo go crashing through the ornamental gardens– by then I was sure at least one of the henchmen would be chasing after us – and bring the black horse to a slithering, clattering halt in the stableyard itself. I knew exactly where it was, because Dean and Kris had drawn a map of the layout when trying to work out their own plan. The next part would take a bit more in the theatrical line from me, but I felt quite sure I could do it. I'd sob hysterically, say I'd injured my hand trying to stop my runaway horse and that I needed a doctor or an ambulance. To quieten me down the thug would agree to call one, and I'd insist, tearfully of course, that Diablo be put in one of those stables while I waited. He could hardly refuse could he, I'd be a damsel in distress after all, and he wouldn't be suspicious of my motives because it was completely by accident that I'd landed up in Hazelgrove, so I'd hardly be likely to do any snooping.

The more I thought about my plan, the more brilliant it seemed. I'd pretend Diablo was all upset and needed me to calm him down and thuggo would leave me gently weeping into my horse's mane while he went to the house to phone a doctor. That would be my chance. Any sign of a trap door or concealed entrance would surely stand out to someone like me who knows there's one there. If anyone found me hunting around I could pretend to have concussion, I could even try keeling over in a faint. I'd done it once before in a school play so it might just come in handy. The only part that seemed a little hazy was what exactly I'd do when I found the hidden cache of paintings. I could hardly round the Randall gang up single handed so the best thing would be to call the police as soon as I got home. I wouldn't give a thing away to the henchmen, or even Randall himself if I met him, I'd be as cool as a cucumber, telling the doctor that my hand wasn't as bad as

I'd thought and leading my horse out of the yard with a sort of brave dignity. Randall would definitely be there by then. I pictured him huge and glowering with a scarred face and an evil laugh that froze the blood in your veins. He'd get his henchmen to escort me off the grounds and say sneering things about my riding prowess as I limped heroically away. Come to think of it, I mustn't limp, it was my hand that was supposed to hurt.

Then, back to Deepdene, dial 999 and the police would swoop without Randall and his gang having any inkling I'd discovered their secret. Kris would come charging up from Hazelgrove agog with the news that the art thieves had been arrested and when Dean got back from his long day prison visiting I'd be able to tell him Randall had confessed everything and his dad would be released and home in time for Christmas. I must admit I spent most of the time basking in the imaginary glory of Dean's gratitude, the gleam in his eyes, the feel of his fingers as he clasped my hand – ooh it was going to be lovely! Thinking back, I realise I should have spent longer working on the plan itself rather than the result, especially thinking out all the things that could possibly go wrong with it. On the other hand if I'd done that I'd never have gone through with it, because as I was about to find out, as ideas go, mine was probably the worse one EVER.

Anyway, trembling with excitement, I somehow stumbled through Tuesday morning's lesson, getting about a hundred reprimands from Miss Crabtree because I made so many mistakes. It was well after ten by the time she gave up and stomped off to the jeep, her back rigid with irritation. Being rubbish at my riding lesson was the first thing that I hadn't planned for my plan, but that was down to nerves, and it was only the start. Next on the agenda was my supposed runaway dash across our field and Diablo's giant leap across the hedge. The black horse set off at a sedate canter. I hadn't gone any faster on him since the day of the genuine runaway, and he seemed surprised when I asked him to quicken his pace. We were now galloping straight for the thorny hedge which looked enormous. High and wide and very, very prickly. I hadn't done any jumping apart from the odd ditch or low wall and, whereas I knew theoretically what to do, in practice I took one look at that hedge and my legs turned to jelly. Diablo sensibly interpreted this as don't jump and merely galloped in a nice wide arc back the way we'd come. I tried one more approach and the hedge looked, if anything, even less inviting, so in the end we came to a halt while I did a rethink. Eventually, by prowling the whole length of our perimeter, I found a nice lowish dip in the level, rode Diablo at it, closed my eyes, tried to recall all the aids to impulsion I'd been taught and to my utter surprise, sailed over the top to land, cantering easily, on the Hazelgrove side!

I patted Diablo's neck excitedly, telling him how wonderful he was and how sorry I was if I'd got it wrong and jabbed his mouth or anything. Then I remembered he was supposed to be bolting so I let the reins flop a bit, screamed rather squeakily and hurtled towards the beautiful ornamental gardens. Diablo, who was probably scared by the bouncing, yelling idiot on his back, did a great job of panic stricken flight. We'd attracted the attention I'd expected, but instead of one henchman there were three! Two of them chased us, trying to turn us off to the side, while the other one, who'd appeared some way in front, started sprinting purposefully towards the stable yard. His intention was obvious, he was going to get there before us and slam the gate shut, totalling ruining the central point of my plan. Forgetting all my riding lessons, I unceremoniously dug my heels into Diablo's side and urged him on. My wonderful horse was too polite to do what he should have done at such treatment and buck me off. He laid his ears back but surged forward across the immaculate green lawn and through a couple of expensively planted flower beds. Number three henchman was just ahead now, running like a hare towards the yard.

To my horror I saw he was yelling into a mobile phone as he went, something else I hadn't figured on. Still it was too late to turn back and I might still find a chance to look round if only I could reach that yard before he did.

The direct route was impeded by an imposing rockery, ornate chunks of granite fashioned into a mound standing at least a metre and a half high. I wanted to go round it, but knew I'd lose precious seconds if I did, so, crouching like a demented monkey halfway up Diablo's neck I roared "Hup!" and my brilliant boy flew through the air again. I'd forgotten to keep screaming to maintain the being-run-away-with myth, but the involuntary yell I gave when we did that jump was full of genuine terror. We were now ahead of all the racing henchmen and all I had to do was stop the wonderful black horse. I tried to recall the half halt, decided the circumstances weren't appro-priate and just leaned back and shouted "Whoa, WHOA!" Poor Diablo, probably utterly confused and fed up with me by now, did his best. He saw the open gate leading to the yard and slammed the brakes on so hard he managed to stop on the grass outside. Unfortunately I didn't, and found myself shunted right over his head to land in a sprawling heap on the bark chippings surface of the path. I was lucky. Another metre and I'd have gone crashing onto the concrete of the yard itself. I had enough sense left, though I suppose as Dean said later, "that's a matter of opinion", to crawl forward and flop myself down on that concrete so that I'd achieved my objective – I was now inside the stableyard at Hazelgrove.

My feeling of victory was short lived. Within seconds henchman number three was yanking me to my feet, still gabbling into his phone. He managed at the same time to curse me with a selection of swear words that would have made my hair curl if it didn't already. Trembling all over, I tried valiantly to stick to my plan.

"I'm sorry, I'm sorry." My tears were quite real. "My horse ran away with me and jumped our fence into your grounds and – "

"Don't talk rot," number three snarled, only he didn't say rot. "You rode that thing deliberately across the gardens. What the hell d'you think you're playing at?"

"Nothing." I carried on lying desperately. "Honestly, I'm not a very good rider and he just took off with me and I couldn't stop him. I'm Stacey Jennings from Deepdene, you know, next door."

I heard the phone in his hands crackle and he listened intently. "We know who you are, Stacey and we also know your great friend Dean Farraday. It was him who put you up to this wasn't it?"

"No, no." At least that was the truth I thought, as I tried to rally my senses. It was no good sticking to the plan and asking for a doctor. Even if they'd consider it they wouldn't have to leave me alone in the stableyard as I'd planned. "Look, please." I tried sniffing forlornly. "My horse must be terrified. Can someone catch him and bring him in here so I can check him over?"

Number three, whose voice I recognised as being the London accent who'd thrown Dean out of Hazelgrove, hesitated for a second or two. Then, turning his head, he barked out orders for the other two to get hold of Diablo.

"Don't think you're getting the chance to snoop around," he sneered at me. "We just don't want the horse galloping back home and raising the alarm. Mr Randall hasn't decided what to do with you yet."

I felt a real shiver of fear then. Dean was right, these were seriously bad people and I was now at their mercy, with no one in the world knowing where I was. I looked round helplessly. The yard looked normal and fairly tidy, though it could have done with a good sweep. There were six looseboxes, their doors shut and bolted, a similarly locked tack room and some kind of store and feed room which was open. I had only a fleeting glimpse of feed bins, bags of shavings, a wheelbarrow, tins of paint, and the usual pitchforks, buckets and shovels. The thug with the London accent grabbed my arm and twisted it uncomfortably behind my back.

"Go on, you." He shoved me hard.

I felt more scared then than I ever had in my life and I stumbled forward onto the path outside the yard.

"Shall I shut the gates Pete?" One of the others was holding Diablo's reins.

Despite my fear I wanted to make sure my horse was all right and I looked him over as best I could.

"You'd better just in case this brat has brought anyone else with he." The thug twisting my arm red. "Shove that black devil in one of the stables and put the lock on when you've done."

"Let me look – " I wanted to check Diablo properly but the one they'd called Pete yanked my arm cruelly.

"You ain't looking at anything." He frogmarched me away and I heard the clatter of my horse's hooves behind me as they took him across the stableyard.

Tears ran freely down my face, not just from the pain in my twisted arm, but for the dread I was feeling that they might do something to Diablo, hurt him in some way. The black horse had done nothing to deserve any of this, it was all my fault and I should never have involved him by coming up with such a stupid, stupid plan. I thought of screaming but as soon as I opened my mouth, Pete's grip tightened and he said, "Don't think about calling for help. There's no one to hear you."

So instead I tried to stop crying, to force myself to show some composure and undermine their confidence that they could deal with me any way they chose. The way the henchmen had reacted when I'd suddenly appeared on Randall's ground, the panic in their voices as they screamed to each other, showed they were seriously rattled. If I could convince them someone knew exactly where I was they might be scared enough to let me go. I was rehearsing a speech where I coolly promised Randall I'd give him and his gang an hour to get out of town before I called the police, when I realised we were approaching Hazelgrove's back door. A shudder ran through me at the thought of meeting the terrifying villain, Randall, and it was all I could do to stop myself bawling again.

Pete hustled me through some kind of utility room and out into the main hall. The house was all garish colours, crimson carpet and green walls which were covered in paintings. I was too frightened and blurry eyed to take them all in but I could see a lot of them were of horses, mostly in the style Dean always dismissed contemptuously as sentimental chocolatebox. There were several doors leading off the hall, showing glimpses of overfurnished dining and drawing rooms, but the

146

room Pete shoved me into was almost bare. There was a single high window, a pile of something covered with a sheet, two straight-backed chairs and one of those swivel lamps you usually see on a desk. It was almost like a cell or, I thought with another shudder, an interrogation room. I had hardly any time to take in the implication that that might have before I heard a horrible soft tread approaching along the hall. Pete, who'd let go of my arm at last, was standing in the doorway.

He craned his neck, then said with a vicious grin, "Right, Stacey Jennings. This'll soon sort you out. Here comes Mr Randall."

I closed my eyes, the vision of the huge man whose scarred and ugly face I'd pictured a thousand times, flashed into my terrified mind. The footsteps halted and I knew when I opened my eyes again I'd be face to face with the arch criminal, Hazelgrove's notorious Mr Randall.

CHAPTER THIRTEEN

I GRITTED MY TEETH, told myself not to be such a wimp, and opened my eyes. Honestly, if I hadn't been holding onto the back of one of the chairs I'd have fallen over. Laughing. The demon Randall, now I was staring straight at him, was just about my height, with a small pinched face and pinkish eyes. He was thin, his sandy hair was balding and he looked more like a depressed insurance clerk than the international master criminal I'd imagined.

I suppressed a nervous giggle and said in what I hoped was a firm voice, "About time too Mr Randall. I hope you're going to do something about the appalling way I've been treated by your – your employees. My horse ran away with me and – "

"Shut up." His voice was low and vicious, matching my concept of him much more than his appearance. He turned his head and looked at Pete. "You've searched the grounds for Farraday have you?"

The thug nodded. "She seems to be on her own. We've got the horse, no one knows she's here."

"Yes they do," I butted in frantically. "Miss Crabtree was giving me a riding lesson. She'll have raised the alarm by now."

"The old dame left earlier." Pete knew I was bluffing. "And Jennings went out just after eight. He's not back and the mother's at the beauty parlour."

I was silent, shaken at the level of surveillance Deepdene seemed to be under.

"And where's the kid?" Randall's piggy little eyes were darting back and forth.

"Don't know." Pete looked worried at admitting it. "He didn't come into work this morning."

I realised it was Dean they were talking about and with a blinding flash understood why they'd been watching us. It must have shaken them badly when my dad gave Dean the job. They probably banked on his reputation, plus the fact he'd been fired from his job, preventing him from getting any sort of work locally. Having the son of Jake Farraday at such close quarters must have made them very, very nervous.

I tried another bluff. "Dean's at the police station now. He's telling them all about your little game. They're probably surrounding the place right now."

"I told you to shut up." Randall looked rattled though. "You lot don't know anything."

"Oh yes we do." In a fit of inspiration I yanked the sheet which was covering, as I'd suspected, twenty or thirty canvasses stacked against the wall. "We know all about this."

Randall turned away, a bored sneer on his ratty features. "As I said, you know nothing. Lock her in here, Pete, till we've checked everything out, then she can go, she's got nothing that anyone would believe."

They both sneered again and walked away. I wasn't so much scared by now as furious, and as usual I went too far.

"Oh yeah," I called childishly. "Well I'll tell you what I do know." I stared round the bare room wildly, my eyes lighting again on the stack of paintings. The top one was a rather soppy portrait of a floppy-maned Arab stallion so I yelled, "I know all about the painted horse, that's what!"

The change in Randall was dramatic and frightening. He whipped round, his already pasty face now chalk white, his pale eyelashes flickering rapidly. He crossed the room in two strides and grabbed both my arms roughly. The one Pete had twisted still hurt and I squealed and tried to pull away but he shook me like a rag doll.

"How the hell? – " To my relief he let go and turned furiously back to Pete. "You said she didn't see anything!"

"She didn't, boss, honest." Pete looked almost as scared as me. "I swear she didn't."

Randall called him some really foul names and said, "We can't risk her getting out now. Lock her in the attic, then we'll have to sort this mess out right away."

Pete immediately got me in an armlock again and pushed and shoved me up the main two flights of stairs, then opened a door and dragged me up another narrow wooden set leading to the very top of the house. He unlocked the door at the top and practically threw me inside. I stumbled into the gloom and fell over something. It hurt and I sobbed miserably, hearing the door slam and the sound of a key turning behind me. I could only sit where I'd landed and cry for a while. Me and my big mouth. If I'd just stayed quiet they'd have let me go quite soon and even if they hadn't there was at least a chance of escaping from that ground floor room. But now – I wiped my eyes and looked around at my new prison. It was quite a big attic, full of the usual junk, boxes of old clothes, broken lamps and piles of books. There was a small window at the far end,letting in enough light for me to make out the shapes of tea chests and the odd discarded ornament. There were no pictures that I could see, not of anything, let alone of painted horses.

"Why did I go and say that?" I told myself off, still sniffing. "Obviously the forgery or theft, or whatever it was Dean's father stumbled into, was all about a horse painting. Miss C said Randall had a huge collection of them."

I shuffled forward cautiously and peered out of

the window. It was just about big enough to climb out of, but it was three floors up in Hazelgrove's eaves, there were no convenient drainpipes to shin down and the nearest tree was at least three metres from the house. All I could do was try opening the window and yelling. My voice sounded little and tinny even to me and I could tell the wind was just carrying it harmlessly away, and in the opposite direction from Deepdene too. I craned forward as far as I dare to look out. I could see the lavish gardens, and noted with malicious satisfaction that even from this far up I could spot the devastation Diablo's galloping hooves had caused. The stableyard wasn't visible and I knew Kris and the rest of Lovall's men were working far away, right over at the back of the paddock, he'd said. I was deeply regretting not telling him about my plan of course. He was so clever and, despite all his teasing and clowning, I felt he'd be a great person to have on your side in a crisis. Thinking about him, I wondered why Randall had tolerated having him work at Hazelgrove when the man was clearly so worried by anyone who had a connection with Dean.

"Surely they must have realised Dean and I have been going round to the cottage most nights to see him?" I pondered, then realisation dawned. Pete and the others had probably seen us all right, but they'd have been under the impression it was

152

Miss Crabtree we were visiting. "And when Kris came to Deepdene he nearly always got a lift in her jeep," I remembered. "So despite all their spying on us, the Randall henchmen don't realise we have a friend working right here."

It was a pleasing thought for a minute or two but it didn't really get me anywhere. I couldn't think of a way of getting a message to Kris. There were no handy carrier pigeons on the roof and of course today was the first time the faithful Jack wasn't around. I imagined myself tying a note to his collar and sending him for help, though quite how I'd get him down to the ground remained a mystery. Time was ticking by. My twisted arm hurt and my knees stung where I'd fallen off Diablo then been thrown into this horrible attic. Diablo. I started worrying about him again. What if – there was a terrific commotion from outside the attic door and I sprang nervously to my feet. It sounded as though someone else was being dragged up the uncarpeted stairs and whoever it was, was putting up more of a fight than I had. The key turned noisily, the door flew open and there was Kris, struggling and kicking in his attempt to get away from Pete and the biggest of the other henchmen. Pete, I was delighted to see, had a split lip and the beginnings of a whacking great black eye. He gave Kris one last vicious kick and sent him crashing across the floor, to crack his head against the packing case that had tripped me up. Both men snarled something, then the door was slammed again and the key not only turned but taken out afterwards.

"Kris!" I dodged through the junk to reach him and knelt anxiously by his side. "Kris, are you hurt? Oh Kris, talk to me."

He lifted his bruised and battered face. "Hi Stace. What's a nice girl like you doing in a dump like this?"

"You fool." I touched his poor face and bit my lip to stop from crying again. "Oh Kris you ARE hurt and it's all my fault."

"You should see the other guy." He grinned crookedly and winced a little. "So, tell me Miss Jennings just what you've been up to. I notice you chose the day your knight in shining armour wasn't around to rescue you. Dean's going to be awfully mad I was the one to save you."

I didn't like to point out that he not only hadn't saved me but had also been caught and locked in an attic himself. Instead I said, "How did you know I was here? And why did they beat you up?"

"I'd sneaked off from the tree felling and was hanging round hoping for a chance to get in the stableyard when all hell broke loose and you and Diablo came bombing across Randall's precious garden." He chuckled at the memory. "For a minute I actually thought you were being run

154

away with, then the thuggos came sprinting out and I heard one of them yelling he'd been watching you try to jump the hedge."

"Damn!" I felt really silly.

"I cottoned on right away what you were up to, but I couldn't do anything, not with there being three of them. I saw them march you off to the house and I was going to go for help but they started searching round so I had to hide."

"They were making sure no one knew where I was," I admitted. "I tried to pretend – oh all sorts."

"I can imagine," he said drily. "Your acting ability is quite marvellous I think. The pretend fall from Diablo was particularly convincing."

"Thank you Kris." I smiled sweetly, knowing he was being funny.

"Anyway, after a while all Randall's lot came pouring out of the house and a lot of yelling and shouting went on. They'd put Diablo in one of the stables, then they ran down to the paddock and brought up two of the horses from there, the light bay and the skewbald."

"What on earth for?" It didn't make sense for them to be moving horses into the yard after I'd told them I knew about their cache of paintings.

"I heard enough to work out the reason." Kris's dark face was serious for once. "They said they were going to load the bay and the black devil into the horse box. I don't know where the other one was going but it was clear Diablo was going to be driven off for several miles then let loose on a stretch of heath or maybe even a beach somewhere."

"Why? My poor darling horse, he might get injured, run onto a road, anything!" I was nearly screaming with horror.

"They couldn't care less about that," Kris said grimly. "The idea is that once your horse is found, riderless but still saddled and bridled, everyone will think you've fallen off and are lying injured somewhere. The search would be concentrated on the area where Diablo is found, taking all the attention away from Hazelgrove and giving Randall a chance to get rid of the evidence against him."

"Evidence – what evidence?" I was totally confused. "There are a lot of paintings in an empty study downstairs, but I still think the stolen ones must be in the stableyard. Randall thought I'd seen them, he went absolutely berserk when I said I knew about it all."

"What exactly did you say?" Kris looked at me and wiped away some blood from his face.

I tried to recall the precise words that had sent the man into such a fiendish temper. "I think it was 'I know all about the painted horse'," I said slowly and Kris slapped his leg with satisfaction.

"I thought so. While they were bringing the

horse box into the yard and sorting out the horses, I was hiding in that store room place. The door was open, you probably saw inside it did you?"

"Yes," I agreed, baffled.

"Tell me what you saw." He now had a smug I've-solved-the-mystery-and-you-haven't expression on his battered face.

I shrugged irritably. "I don't know. Feed bins and brushes. A wheelbarrow."

"Anything else?"

I racked my brains. "Shavings. Oh, and some tins of paint."

"There's a clever girl." Kris patted my head. "That's what Randall was afraid you'd seen. While I was crouching behind the door, Pete came in and picked up a tin. Only it wasn't paint this time, it was paint remover." He stopped as though he'd said it all.

"So?" I could have hit him if there were any bits of him that hadn't been already.

"So, Stacey Jennings, what this is all about, the thing that's turned Randall into a nervous recluse and caused Jake Farraday to be set up for a crime he didn't do, is exactly what you said – a painted horse."

I thought he'd gone mad and told him so.

"Don't you get it? Look I'll give you a major clue. I'll bet anything you like when Dean quizzes his dad about what he saw that night, Jake will say he only saw a horse being taken from a stable and put into a field. A light bay horse, Stacey."

I decided to humour him and try to be logical. "OK. So he saw the light bay horse that is now being driven off with my Diablo."

"And what's that horse supposed to be?" Kris asked patiently. "Remember, Randall told Mr Lovall all about him."

"The bay's going to be his event horse," I said wearily. "Though Miss C says Randall's got no chance because neither he or the horse are any good. But I still don't see – " I stopped abruptly. "Hey, hang on. Dean's dad couldn't have seen the light bay horse that night. Randall only bought him recently."

"Now you're getting there." Kris went to pat me again but I scowled so fiercely he withdrew his hand. "The horses in the paddock up until a few weeks back were a grey, two dark bays and a skewbald, right?"

"Right. That was the group Dean took photos of, the ones he painted later on. Oh surely that's not the painted horse you mean?"

"In a way it is. When you asked Miss Crabtree what she thought of the painting, she said the skewbald was wrong didn't she, and we all ignored her. But she was quite right – that type of horse – I don't know whether it's a Thoroughbred or a Warmblood, I'm pretty ignorant about that stuff – is always a solid colour, they only ever have a blaze or white socks or something."

"My god!" I stared at him. "The skewbald was really a light bay who'd been painted! For some reason Randall disguised him as a coloured horse, literally painted on sweeps of white to make him look like – like – "

"Like a circus horse. That's how they'd have smuggled him out from wherever they stole him. Tony Cinquetti would have done the actual stealing, on Randall's orders, then moved him with the rest of his performing troop across the states and over to England. They brought him here and thought they were safe, so they cleaned the paint off him and put him out in the field with the other three when no one was around to comment on the arrival of a new one."

"And that was the night Dean's father was doing his bit of poaching," I breathed. "So he saw – "

"All he saw was what he said, a horse being put into a field. But Randall wasn't sure how long Farraday had been hanging round. He might have seen a skewbald go into the yard and a light bay come out. Whatever happened Randall didn't want anyone listening to Jake's story about a horse so he set up the break-in and the assault on his thug so that nobody would believe anything Jake said."

"My god!" I said again. "So – so why did Randall buy that other light bay? And why did he steal the first one in the first place?" It was all far too clever for me.

"I reckon the first one, the stolen one that they painted, is something really special. He's probably a top-class event horse in America and Randall, as we know, is completely obsessive about becoming a winner in dressage or whatever. After the upset with Jake Farraday, my guess is Randall had to have a complete rethink and realised he couldn't suddenly turn up at competitions with this wonderful horse without people asking where it had come from. So he had it repainted again, just in case anyone checked, then very publicly bought the second bay, a mediocre performer, which he announced to everyone he was going to turn into a star. He didn't want anyone snooping around, so he stopped inviting people to watch him in his fancy manege, and made sure no one went near the stables or paddock to get a close look at 'the skewbald'."

"But he's got loads of money. Why did he have to steal bay number one in the first place?" I repeated. "Why not just buy him?"

"I don't suppose he was for sale," Kris said simply. "But that wouldn't stop Randall would it? If you can't buy it – steal it, that's how the man thinks. Now all he has to do is get rid of the second bay, clean the paint off the skewbald, and turn up at a competition with the horse he's supposed to have schooled into a surefire winner."

I thought of the horsebox, which would no doubt be trundling off with my beloved Diablo and the poor, innocent "second bay", even as we spoke. "Oh Kris, what a dirty, dirty trick. And there's nothing we can do to stop him."

CHAPTER FOURTEEN

To my surprise Kris's face broke into the widest, wickedest grin I'd ever seen – even on him. "Not quite true. Why d'you think Pete and his pal gave me such a hiding? Not just because they caught me, it was more what they caught me doing."

He paused and I said, because he obviously expected me to say, "What were you doing?"

"I crawled under the horsebox and cut the lead to the starter motor," he chuckled ruefully. "It was a pity they nabbed me before I could get away and call the police, but one thing's for sure – that horsebox isn't going anywhere."

I hugged him. I just couldn't help it. "So Diablo's safe! Oh Kris, you are wonderful."

"It's about time you said that. The trouble is Randall will have sent for a mechanic with a new lead. They won't risk hiring a box, obviously, but I don't know how long it will take for a new lead to be fitted. I'm going to have to get out of here and raise the alarm before they get mobile again."

"It's impossible. They've taken the door key out and the window's no good." I watched him as he wrenched up the old sash-cord frame.

He looked out for a moment and then said, unexpectedly, "Is that the church steeple at

Hembury, in the distance?"

"I think so," I said, mystified. "Why?"

"Oh, it's just that it's one of the few things my mother ever mentioned. She came from round here originally, you know – that was my main reason for heading this way. She never came back after she married my dad. I don't think the few family she had were keen on her marrying a circus performer."

He'd never really talked about his parents before, and although I found now to be rather a strange time, I was sensitive enough to be interested.

"But you haven't spent all your life with the circus in America, have you?"

"Oh no. Mum wanted me to have a proper education, so I was at school in England while they toured. It was when they were both killed in a car crash that I joined Grandad. He was willing to teach me but I guess it was a bit late for me to learn the family act and I just didn't make the grade. Poor old Grandad Marenga. When he died there was no one left and he knew it was the end of our circus history. In a way I was relieved I didn't have to pretend anymore. I wasn't cut out for the life and I certainly wasn't good enough to be a top-class performer. Still," he withdrew his head from the open window and went on briskly, "I was good enough to do what I intend now.

Stacey, see if you can find a decent length of rope amongst all this junk."

"Rope?" He had me baffled again. "You're not thinking of lowering yourself down to the ground? They'll spot you before you're halfway and beat you up again."

"They won't see me at al." He was searching through a trunk, tossing things all over the place in his haste.

I joined in, tipping out the contents of the tea chest we'd both crashed into. "What about this?" I held up a length of sturdy looking nylon line.

Kris examined it critically. "Just about long enough I think. It's about five or six metres would you say?"

"Yes." Nowhere near long enough to reach the ground, I was thinking, but Kris was already tying one end firmly round one of the supporting beams.

"Right." He sprang lightly onto the window ledge. "Here's where my lassoing expertise comes in. I hope."

I couldn't see exactly where he was throwing the other end of the rope, though I could see he'd made a professional looking slip-knot loop in it.

He made several attempts, patiently coiling up the line every time it fell short and carefully aiming again. On the fifth go I heard him give a satisfied grunt and watched as he pulled the line taut and refastened it firmly round the beam.

"Mm." He was now staring down at his feet. "Welly boots are not the ideal footwear. My socks will be better, not ideal, but better."

"Better for what?" I was getting worried. I still had no idea what he planned to do but I knew, I just knew it was going to be something crazy.

He slid back into the attic and pulled the boots off, rubbing the underneath of his socks and inspecting them critically. I took a peek out of the window and wished I hadn't. The thin rope, stretched as taut as a steel rod, was now attached to a branch of the nearest tree. For the first metre or so it ran just above the red tiles of Hazelgrove's roof, but for at least three and a half metres it hung suspended over the sheer drop to the ground below.

"Kris! You're going to crawl out and hang from that rope to work your way across to the tree? You must be mad. They'll hear you. They'll see you. The rope will break. You mustn't – "

"I'm not." He gently pushed me aside and sprang back onto the window ledge. "The Flying Marengas never, never crawl. And we don't hang either."

To my unspeakable horror he got lightly to his feet, took a few seconds to adjust his balance, then ran, actually ran straight out across the roof! I nearly screamed, had to clap my hand over my mouth as, eyes popping, I watched his stockinged feet race confidently across the nylon rope which stretched over the gaping void between house and tree. In less time than it takes to say it, he'd reached the branch, held it and vaulted neatly to grasp the main trunk. My hand was still covering my mouth, which was just as well because I felt like being very, very sick, but I did manage to wave feebly at him with the other one. His return wave was more like a victory salute and I prayed and prayed that no one had seen his miraculous escape and there'd be nobody waiting to pounce when he climbed down to the ground. I brought my head and shoulders back into the room and slid slowly down the wall, still in a state of shock. I just sat like that, legs stuck out in front of me, eyes staring vacantly at the junk filled attic until the sound of police sirens came faintly through the window. It was just the sound I needed.

Agog to see Randall's comeuppance, I strained as far out of the window as I could, hearing tanta- lising sounds of running feet and shouted curses. There were police whistles too, and the noise of German Shepherd dogs barking. I found myself hoping Randall and Pete had made a run for it and were being pursued by the biggest, fiercest dogs in the whole of the Dorset police force. After a while the commotion outside slowed down and then everything went quiet. I still couldn't see a thing and I even considered climbing out onto the roof and holding onto Kris's rope to get a better view. Luckily I didn't have to – the wonderful sound of the key turning in the attic door brought me rushing across the room.

A very tall, slightly dishevelled looking policeman smiled at me and said calmly, "There you are, miss. A friend of yours said we'd find you here."

I nearly fell into his arms and when I saw Kris, standing proudly at the front door watching a big black car drive Randall and his thugs away, I nearly fell into his too.

Instead I said coolly, "Call yourself a Flying Marenga do you?"

His smile dropped a little. "Why? What would you call me?"

"I think knight in shining armour springs to mind." I smiled a bit soppily and he laughed out loud and said, "Well for goodness' sake don't tell Dean!"

We had an awful lot to tell Dean without that. By the time he got home, tired and dispirited from his visit, Kris and I were well on the way to being totally over the top about the whole thing. My Mum, who was in a state of shock similar to mine when I saw Kris's tight-rope act, insisted on giving us all "proper cooked meal". I think she felt it might calm us all down but we were beyond that

I'm afraid. Poor Dean, he could hardly take it all in. Obviously nothing had yet been done about releasing his dad, but the police assured him it was just a matter of formality. Being able to arrest Randall on a firm charge of theft, with the stolen goods still on him (that's the bay who used to be a skewbald – the painted horse you know) meant they could now search his house for evidence of a million and one other crimes they'd suspected him of for years.

"There are some really dirty deeds the police are going to be able to prove," my dad told us with great relish. "The art gallery in Barringford is, as you all thought, just a front, a way of hiding crooked deals under a legitimate business."

"I just knew no one could make big money out of the kind of paintings that Randall's taste runs to." Dean curled his lip in distaste. "All those pretty horses and cute kittens in baskets."

I quite like cute kitten pictures but now wasn't the time to say so. Until Kris had spelled out the real solution to the mystery I'd remained convinced it was all to do with art theft and hidden paintings so I didn't want to remind anyone how dopey I'd been. Anyway I had my work cut out to get back in the good books of both Dean and my dad. Dad had been quite shocked at the part I'd played, but he was gradually getting over it and was wholeheartedly enjoying celebrating the clearing of Jake Farraday's name.

"Your father will always be proud you never doubted him and that you worked so hard to prove it," he told Dean.

"It was Stacey and Kris who came up with the proof though." Dean looked rueful. "I'd never have gone away today if I'd known what your daughter was up to, Mr Jennings." He'd confirmed what Kris had deduced – that it was a light bay horse his dad saw being put into the field, but he hadn't been able to make any sense of it. "It didn't occur to me that it was the wrong colour. Yet I'd thought from the start the mystery must have something to do with the horses. That's why I took those photos. I should have spotted that the 'skewbald' I made a sketch of wasn't correct."

"You've got more of an artist's eye than a horseman's, that's why," Dad said. "You painted exactly what you saw. I think the first thing your dad should do when he gets home is sort out a place at art college for you."

"When my dad gets home," Dean repeated, obviously liking the sound of the words. "It shouldn't be long, the detective inspector told me 'off the record' that Pete is singing like a bird."

"That means he's confessing, does it dear?" Mum was trying to keep up.

"It sure does." Kris, with his bruised face and

split knuckles, looked more devilish than ever. "And he's putting the finger on his boss for just about everything he's ever done. They've promised him a lighter sentence if he cooperates and my guess is he's pretty sick of the treatment he's been getting from Randall, so Pete's enjoying making sure the guy goes down for a long, long time."

"Great." Dean hadn't said much directly to me. Despite the outcome he was still mad I'd taken so many risks.

I tried to make him look at me by saying, "Ooh, you didn't hear the best punch line to all this, did you? Mr Lovall and his men carried on working on the new sand school right up till lunch time. They told the policeman who found them that they'd heard sirens and a bit of a rumpus but thought they'd 'best carry on with the job'."

Dean joined in the laughter, which showed he was starting to forgive me, then he frowned. "Why was Randall building that second schooling ring?" he asked. "Does anyone know?"

"It was part of the paranoia he felt about the stolen horse getting spotted," Kris said, having, as usual, worked it all out. "After your dad saw the horse without its paint, Randall was dead scared someone might put two and two together and come looking for it. The sand school was so tucked away no one would ever see it was a skewbald

170

who was so brilliant at dressage, not the light bay horse Randall had bought."

"Why didn't he just get rid of the second one?" I wanted to know. "Why keep both of them?"

"Same reason. He was scared of someone believing Jake's story and investigating the light bay. If somebody official asked to check out the horse Jake said he'd seen, then Randall would just trot up the second one, which although similar to the stolen horse isn't the stolen horse if you follow me."

"It's all too complicated for me," my mum complained. "You really must have an awfully good brain to have worked it all out, Kris."

I'm sure she nearly added "despite the way you look" but she's much too polite and kind to do that. We carried on talking and eating and laughing for what seemed like hours. It was wonderful to see Dean looking so happy, to hear Kris's clever deductions and to know that my adored, brilliant Diablo was safe and unharmed in his own stable. Miss Crabtree, who'd carefully made no comment whatsoever when she heard about the black horse's part in my dreadful plan, was taking charge of Randall's horses for the time being. The painted horse had indeed, of course, been stolen. The police in America had already informed the real owner, who'd been scouring her own country for him, unaware that he'd been whisked away in the midst of a troop of visiting coloured circus horses. The police were also hot on the heels of Tony Cinquetti, who, Kris said cheerfully, would be very glad to incriminate Randall, rather than take the blame for the theft himself. The woman who'd had the horse stolen was a top competition rider over in the States and she was flying in straight away to identify her immensely valuable animal. Kris said Miss Crabtree would be bound to sort out what was best for the others.

"She's a real diamond my Miss C," he told us proudly. "She took the whole story in her stride, just tutted about Stacey jumping the hedge and opened her eyes a bit wide when I got to where I high wired my way out of the attic. Funny enough, she says she'd been doing some investigations of her own and that she got the results today as well, but I won't know what that's about until I see her tonight.

"Maybe she's been suspicious of Randall too," I suggested. "She didn't ever like him that's for certain."

But it wasn't Hazelgrove's master criminal Miss Crabtree had been finding out about. Dean and I met up with Kris the next day and for once his dark eyes looked dazed and he was, for him, almost inarticulate.

"You know Miss C," he began awkwardly, then took a deep breath. "I'll tell you the way she told me. 'I saw a likeness straight away Kris, although of course your colouring is all from your father. So I've been making enquiries, and at last the American authorities have come up with the information I required'." He paused and looked at us almost helplessly. "Guys, I'm not alone in the world. She's my cousin or my second cousin once removed or something. She knew my mother and everything."

"Who? Miss C!" Dean and I gasped simultaneously.

"You're related to Miss Crabtree!" I couldn't help it, I just started giggling and Kris got quite mad.

"What's so funny? She's great."

"She certainly is and so are you." I pulled myself together. "But in – sort of different ways."

"No wonder she took to you so quickly." Dean was quite relieved, it was something that had always bugged him. "So does that mean you'll stay?"

"Oh yeah." Kris smiled very proudly. "It makes all the difference, having family."

"And you'll carry on working for Mr Lovall?" It would be great having him around still, I thought contentedly.

"Well no." He looked quite sheepish again. "My – cousin thinks I've got a good brain, just like your Mom does, Stacey. She wants me to enrol at college. I'm pretty keen myself, even thinking of getting enough qualifications to go in for law, maybe."

"Phew," I whistled in mock admiration. "A pair of real high fliers you're turning out to be. I thought my friends were a couple of thickie labourers but they're turning into an artist and a lawyer before my very eyes."

We were in the hayloft again and they both buried me under piles of straw till I yelled for mercy. I sat up, picked a few strands out of my mouth, and watched them clowning around the barn. They were both feeling on top of the world, with plenty to look forward to, and were showing every sign of becoming good friends too. I was pleased, it made life very entertaining for me having them both around. I stared dreamily out of the window and did a little future planning for myself. Both Miss C and Diablo were being very forgiving about the appalling horsemanship I'd shown yesterday, but I was determined that once I got to grips with flatwork, learning to jump properly was an urgent priority. So, I'd get on with learning basic equitation, then dressage and jumping, in order to think seriously about competing, but what would I do for a career – ?

"I'll probably go to college too" I decided, and grinned happily at the thought. "I'd better get equipped for the job market just in case I don't make the grade as an eventer. Can't expect to be a spoilt little Daddy's girl all my life. And who knows, I might get myself a boyfriend while I'm studying, maybe an artist or even a lawyer!"

As I said to Diablo later on when I told him about all our plans, "Stranger things have happened. Let's face it," I hugged him lovingly, "nothing could be much stranger than a real, live, painted horse!"

HATS